T0131499

ONCO
III AND A HALF

THE MONSTER IS UNMASKED

ANTHONY JANICSKA-BOROSS PhD

BALBOA.
PRESS
A DIVISION OF HAY HOUSE

Balboa Press books may be ordered through booksellers or by contacting:

Balboa Press
A Division of Hay House
1663 Liberty Drive
Bloomington, IN 47403
www.balboapress.com.au
1 (877) 407-4847

Print information available on the last page.

ISBN: 978-1-5043-1743-6 (sc)
ISBN: 978-1-5043-1744-3 (e)

Balboa Press rev. date: 07/25/2019

PREAMBLE.

The Australian Government's Food Administration Division had developed a novel source of food. The research was in response to the World Hunger campaign, which posited that the planet was running out of food, and the mass famines would only worsen as the population continued to grow exponentially.

Food Administration has its operational centre at Maralinga within Woomera, erstwhile nuclear testing base used by Britain in the 1940's, in the Great Victoria Desert.

Over many years of research, Food Admin. Developed a process to grow edible meat from Cattle Stem Cells and rapid-growth Cancer Cells (yes, I did say cancer cells), and put the procedure on a commercial footing.

This is described in the first book, ONCO, where the Cattle conglomerates hatched a plan to wreck the establishment which they considered a threat to the beef food industry. The tragic results were much to their chagrin, and to everyone else's.

In ONCO II, we see a new process plant emerge, near the ruins of the old one. A two-man Desert Patrol had, as one of its duties, the task of periodically checking the ruins. On one of the visits, a growth from the wreckage was noticed, and one of the team tried to pull it out of the crack in the concrete from where it sprouted.

The growth instantly enveloped the Patrolman's hand, and tried to pull him to the crack

After segregation in hospital, the man was found to be suffering from all-invasive cancer, metastasis to the extreme, and eventually he turned into a virtual cancer mass, which was operating his body *as though he himself* was alive. Soon, he tried to escape from the hospital, but was incinerated by an inspector from the AFP, the Australian Federal Police, using a flame-thrower.

A remnant of the weird growth was kept for investigation under laboratory conditions, and this grew into a threatening entity, the behaviour of which tweaked the attention of the Australian Weapons Development Authority. Weapons decided to take over the monstrosity and find some use for it in the Defence Department.

The entity evolved and developed beyond expectations, and possessed intelligence and weird abilities and powers, which made it a budding threat to humanity. This progressed under the control of Colleen Sans, a scientist who developed a strange relationship with Creature, as it became known.

Eventually, the Government tried to actually use Creature for military purposes, but Colleen and Security Officer Frank Vagyoczki escaped the Government Facility and took Creature with them, to a location which they hoped would be kept secret, as explained in ONCO III.

In this present volume, titled ONCO III AND A HALF, the pair together with Creature are located and a chase ensues with many adventures, and an unexpected climax.

AT MARALINGA, THE PREMISES of the Australian Weapons Research and Development Authority.

Jim Mullens was furious. When he got the news of Colleen and Frank absconding, he could hardly contain his rage. And he could not substitute a target for his anger; had he been able to confront Colleen, there would have been unstoppable sparks, perhaps even violence.

Jim, as well as some others, could only see one possibility.
Treason.

His mind worked along very simple lines. There was never an 'if.' Or 'maybe.'

Something was either 'yes' or 'no'. Black or white. Nothing in between.

You may gather that Jim had no perception of *grey*. And this attitude served him well in the past. He always knew what to do, and maybe nine out of ten, he was right in whatever choice he made.

And he was spewing also for another reason; he was the one that originally picked Frank Vagyoczki. He headhunted him from Food Administration, and the AFP, the Australian Federal Police, and being the man he was, he saw the recent incidents as personal failure. Which he could never accept.

His boss, Paul Mitchell, the head of the Weapons Research and Development Authority, was more pragmatic. And unlike Jim, he could see all shades of grey. Not just 60, like the title of the old movie of doubtful contribution to anything but bondage, sex, sadism, and masochism but *all*.

Paul knew from the first that this matter was out of his control, and to attempt to involve himself any more would be doomed to failure. Colleen was one of his well-regarded staff, and Frank was no more nor less than that. But he knew he had to let go of both, and leave others more suited to deal with the issues.

He had a good discussion with Joe Kadas, the Colonel in charge of the subset of the Pine Gap Signals Directorate in the Victoria Desert, who was also 'pissed off' by the loss of his perceived promising assistant Colleen.

Colleen, although only temporarily under Joe's control, was the only connection between the Signals Directorate and world politics, via the Onco entity, named 'Creature' by the Weapons staff, which was an impossibility to decipher. Colleen was the only one that could get this entity to co-operate.

Chief Inspector - soon Commissioner- Bill Bradbury of the Australian Federal Police was dragged again into this scenario. To be honest, he was not very happy about the events that led up to the absconding of Frank and Colleen.

He was not too familiar with Colleen, but Frank was his erstwhile employee, and he was not ecstatic when Frank applied for transfer to Weapons. Frank was doing a good job in the field as an operative, and Bill only let him go as he was personally fond of Frank, and as he understood Weapons would give Frank more opportunities than the AFP could.

And now, instead of being his protégé, Bill had to try and track him down as an adversary. Not a pleasant turn of events. Bill was a formidable opponent, and he knew that Frank would appreciate that. After all, they had a long-term workplace association before the emergence of Onco onto the scene.

There were not a lot of leads. The pair, Colleen and Frank, had covered their tracks well. It was soon found that Colleen sold her car at Alice Springs, and it was well known that Colleen made her last contact from Alice.

WE NOW BREAK INTO our current story, 'ONCO III AND A HALF.'

AFTER THEIR ESCAPE, THE trio, being Colleen, Frank and Creature, simply disappeared from the surface of the earth. *So it seemed.*

The last known positions of each of the three were pinpointed and recorded in the Mainframe Computer system of the AFP. All the trails converged on Alice Springs; Mprtwent in the local Arrente Aborigine language, is in the Red Centre, approximately in the geographical centre of the Continent, and administratively speaking, actually in the Northern Territory.

It has, since the 1960's, been an important Defence Organisation location with the development of Pine Gap Joint Defence Satellite Surveillance Earth Station. The kernel of the Defence Department's Australian Signals Directorate. High security to the utmost.

Alice itself being about half-way between Adelaide and Darwin, had a chequered history. Before the Second World War, it had a loose population of around 500 people, in the form of an isolated settlement, and some drifters, prospectors and itinerant farm workers. Plus of course some aborigines.

During the war, WWII, it was an equally isolated Staging Camp, being as we said between Adelaide and Darwin, but for that very reason, an important focal point in the Continent's geography.

It was the *sole* staging station between Adelaide and Darwin. The military importance of this camp is obvious.

The three fugitives, Colleen, Frank and Creature, left Alice by way of the railway called the Ghan. The Ghan, a trans-continental rail line originally named after the Afghan and Pakistani camel drivers that came to Australia with their camels during the late 19th Century to help explore the vast interior. Just incidentally, the camels have since expanded into a wild continental herd of many thousands. Good breeders, eh?

Not all that much different from the humans of their origin (Central Asia), who may produce upwards of 15 children per family, most of whom will eventually starve or lose their lives due to violence being the product of their ideology. But back on our story;

Along the edge of the Simpson Desert, Alice lies just south of the Tropic of Capricorn.

The choice of escape routes for Colleen, Frank and Creature, were varied. All of them were dangerous (or adventurous, depending on your attitude).

Back to Adelaide, would have been like walking into the jaws of the crocodile. A well-developed and aggressive AFP would be waiting for them.

Up north, towards Darwin, was a better choice. The sparsely populated Northern Territory presented no major specific risks.

East or West, the desert would be a major obstacle to their escape.

The choices boiled down and reduced to straight north, towards the Territory Capital, Darwin. And the Ghan was a convenient route, the only problem being that Bill Bradbury would be well aware of the same aspects as Colleen ad Frank were contemplating.

Frank had close contacts in Darwin going back to his days with the SAS (Special Air Service), and other organisations. This made the decision a lot easier. At Alice, they bought rail tickets to Darwin, and used disguise clothing and make-up at the motel before joining the train.

A couple, with a child in a wicker basket, weren't too obvious.

6   ANTHONY JANICSKA-BOROSS PhD

The child, of course, was Creature. Colleen made sure that it understood all the happenings, and the reason for silence and other covert modes of operation to ensure no detection. Ample baby clothing (benefits of the only used—clothes store in town, run by the Salvation Army – or 'Salvos') was used to mask Creature, and from a moderate distance, it appeared innocent enough.

And so it happened. With the proceeds from the sale of her car, they purchased two tickets to Darwin. Children under 12 travelled free, so the basket containing Creature was exempt. Before soon, they were on their way. Certainly apprehensive, certainly not without fear, but they were at least headed for *some* certainty. Down the track. Or really, *up* the track, as Darwin is as far *up north* as you can accept before hitting the 'Torres Strait'.

Tennant Creek, a gold mining and Aboriginal exposure settlement and Katherine were minor stops along the way, the line finishing at East Arm in Darwin.

In world- terms, Darwin is still basically much like the colonial capital it used to be. But, not to be fooled, it has now also grown to be a mega-city on the back of tourism and Chinese exploitation, plus the US Marine exchange program, thrusting thousands of Americans right into the Australian tropics on a bi-annually rotating basis.

Add the fact that China was leasing Darwin Harbour on an originally 99-year lease, so Darwin was indeed a point of consideration.

Our heroes were picked up at East Arm, and were whisked away to a secret hideout in the City Centre. Frank's connections certainly excelled in their covert operations. The hideout was nicely hidden in the cellars of a major city building, and was well-concealed from prying eyes. There was a complete apartment here, with all facilities and conveniences as needed.

Frank had a location in the nexus Android Web, and he was well equipped to handle security and related issues.

When they were first introduced to the covert location, Collen remarked to herself; 'this is like the dungeon in Weapons Development Authority.' And she was not too far out of place here.

As it felt, this surely was analogous to Weapons. But in reality it was only a Shopping Centre car-park.

The unit; entry and exit were via a small indistinct door fitted into and the same colour as the concrete wall, opening into the car-park itself, which, being a 24-hour facility, was always busy.

And when you want to hide, the busier the better. The door hid a windowless area being the lounge, a study room, a bedroom with an on-suite, then a tiny kitchenette-meals, and a pantry/store room.

They had by now become lovers, partly due to the common cause, and partly to being thrown together in constant contact, not to forget the facts that Colleen was quite pretty, and Frank was an attractive man.

All-in-all, the outcome was inevitable, yet nothing physical occurred during their work together at 'Weapons,' and when they later set up their tiny headquarters in Darwin, the realisation came that there was only one bedroom in the place.

Initially, Frank was content to sleep on the lounge, but he still had to travel through the bedroom to get to the on-suite. And one night, as he came out of the little bathroom, Colleen said, out of the dark; 'Frank, it must be awfully uncomfortable on that lounge. Besides, you keep disturbing my sleep. Why don't you just snuggle up here with me?'

Frank, naturally, being a virile man, although surprised, needed no further encouragement, and of course the expected happened. Colleen was the initiator, but to her credit, she has not had a man in her life since her divorce almost three years ago, and she certainly was not an easy sleep-around hoe.

But although not really in love, they were both very fond of one another, and they were both happy with the new arrangement. Fortunately, the room had a double bed, which made it all possible, as a smaller item would not have accommodated Frank's largish frame.

Creature was located in the study, and it was happy enough to find it had access to Colleen's computer, and her new bookshelf; the old one at the Facility was Government property, and had to be abandoned together with her books and manuals.

She soon replenished her stock of trade and scientific books via the local major Bookseller, Dymocks, at Casuarina Square. And more via e-Bay. A bigger problem was to find a suitable electron microscope, which she felt she needed to continue her private research. And a JPEG Image Capture program.

The microscope she found at the decommissioning sale of the old Darwin Hospital, with its contents separately sold. The Image Grabber was no less difficult to find, and she finally found suitable software on e-Bay, which she had then downloaded from Sydney.

A sturdy 4-drawer filing cabinet, desk and office chair were available from a handy used-furniture store, as were two small fridges, one for household use and the other for specimen storage, also a suitable desk lamp.

She needed a small wash-basin for lab use, and as the study was not connected to the building plumbing waste system, Frank knocked together a make-shift one with the basin discharging into a twenty-litre drum, which of course had to be emptied once a day. Another job for Frank. The water source was just from bottled water.

However, for disposal, a convenient spot for Frank in this was initially the bathroom floor waste drain, which sure came in handy, but soon, it started smelling somewhat.

The waste then was simply tipped down the toilet bowl. As it did not contain biological material, there was no risk to the environment.

All of this and other things depleted their savings somewhat, though fortunately most things they bought had been used stock.

Even the cars Frank bought at Darwin were second hand.

The Building Manager was a friend of Frank's from the olden days, and Frank realised all his and Colleen's old friends and even casual contacts would be investigated by the AFP. It was fortunate for the couple that Frank's old friend was not on the Government radar as the friendship pre-dated Frank's employment with the AFP.

Nevertheless, Frank had to have a serious talk with the Building Manager, and he laid all the cards on the table, with the exception of Creature. That had to remain a secret. The reason for the couple's presence in Darwin as given by Frank to the Building Manager was that Frank and Colleen developed a relationship, which interfered with their work.

(A plausible half-truth, that is the relationship. No truth about interfering with their work.) And to ensure no contamination of the environment, creature had to remain in its globe, which was no different for it than what it was already used to. So Frank's friend never even had to set eyes on it.

The only problem was the matter of the aerial waste emissions from the sphere. But they were in luck to the extent that the building was supplied with cooking gas, and the little flat they shared had an outlet with a little gas convection heater, which Frank soon converted so the flue was utilised as a means to burn any emission before it was released into the atmosphere. All of Creature's waste was gaseous, so the setup was functional.

Why a flat in the tropical Northern Territory became originally fitted with a gas heater was a total mystery to Colleen and Frank, but they were glad to utilise it as a very fortunate adjunct to their efforts.

IN THE MIDDLE OF one night, a shriek. Colleen woke first followed closely by Frank. Colleen said; 'Frank, did you hear that?' Frank immediately responded; 'If you mean that shriek, yes, of course I heard it. How could anyone miss it?' Colleen said; 'do you think it was something in the car park?

Then another shriek. And it was obvious to both Colleen and Frank that it came from *inside* their unit.

Frank said; 'Creature!' And, as one, they rushed out of the bedroom and into the study.

They confronted Creature, hanging in the half-light. Colleen always left some measure of light on every night, so that Creature could read, manoeuvre the computer, lift books out of the book-case, all by remote psychokinesis, and do all things it wanted. Except release from its globe. Not that it really needed the half-light even; it could operate in almost total darkness.

Creature was obviously upset, they could feel the emanations. Then Frank glanced at the VU meter which via a microphone and amplifier continually measured sound levels in the study. The meter that was modified by Frank to monitor sound producing a tracing for the last five minutes constantly, as a sine wave graph with converted output to the computer.

An audio-engineer would have been proud of Frank's achievement; a view of the screen would show you the history of any sound continuously from five minutes before the present.

In this case, a quick glance confirmed what was always on the horizon with Creature; is the sound *real* or is it another emanation from Creature? As it turned out, the 'shriek' sound was inaudible. No output to the VU meter. It was just a mental output from Creature, picked up direct by the brains of Colleen and Frank, as it would have been by any other person in range.

Next question was fired by Colleen; 'what's the matter, Creature?'

Creature responded; 'Colleen, what are these horrible lumps growing from the bases of my vertices? What is happening?'

Colleen said; 'settle down, Creature, till I can investigate.'

And investigate she did. First, she examined Creature visually, which was not much help, as the wall of the globe stopped her from getting close enough. However, she convinced Creature to press one of its vertices against the Plexiglas, and with the aid of a hand-held magnifier, she could ascertain that the lumps were not imaginary, but real. All of Creature's five vertices displayed the same appearance as to the lumps.

Colleen then proceeded to replay Judy's DVD's which contained the shots of Hans prior to his horrible death. Also, the conversations amongst the scientists well before that time, when the 'buds' first appeared on Hans, and the remarks surrounding the event. Even Frank's not-so-funny comments of that time to which Brian Archwald took exception.

Like; 'will the 'buds' fall off Hans and then would we have little Hans's running around the floor?'

Whereupon Colleen, who was not present at the meetings where Margaret Wheatley put forth the theory (OncoIII) about hydra reproduction, and immortality, shot a disbelieving glance at Frank. The latter protested that it was only a joke at the time, and that he had already apologised then.

Not that any of that was any help to Hans. The apologies, that is. By the time of this writing, he was well and truly gone (Onco ll).

In the interim, whilst all this investigation was taking place, Creature remained hanging on tenterhooks (figuratively, although it was already hanging on vertices, we may say).

At the end, Colleen sat down with Frank and they discussed the implications of what could be happening. Colleen put to Frank; 'it may be having babies, so to speak, as an analogue. We still have no idea about its gender (if any) sexuality (if any) or any idea as to reproduction (if any).'

Frank said; 'Colleen, we must allay Creature's fears while we investigate further. We don't want it in a panic about its possible fate.'

And so they spoke (communicated) with Creature, and honestly told it that the best they could offer was that they would remain on the track, and advise Creature of any relevant information they uncovered.

Creature accepted the inevitable, and was intelligent enough to go along with it. At least it was no longer in a screaming panic.

AND CREATURE CONTINUED GROWING. More than that, it was beginning to develop features more common to humans than to anything else. We will recall that Hans, before his sad demise, started to develop buds, which one scientist likened to those on the hydra, a small aquatic animal that was deemed immortal as it grew buds to propagate itself, which then dropped off to start new animals, the original animal never ceasing life.

Well, as we said above, and much to his alarm, Creature similarly started to grow them. Whereas Hans' life was sadly cut short, Creature was still very much alive and, as we said, growing.

Within a month at Darwin, its weight exceeded one kilo, which meant Frank had to search for resources to build it another globe. But the buds, they were a mystery as in Hans, then also so in Creature.

In Hans' case, the buds were pushing against the corium, the inner layer of skin. In the case of Creature, they were also doing the same. But whereas Hans died before a resolution of these growths, Creature was developing them beyond the "Hans stage."

And whereas in the hydra they dropped off, in the case of Creature, they grew firmly anchored, like the pre-cursors of organs or extremities of a foetus do whilst still *in-utero*. Stem cells pre-develop into organs and limbs. In the case of Hans, an autopsy, had it been possible, may have revealed the secrets of the buds.

However, as we know, Hans was killed and incinerated before such investigations could happen.

In the case of Creature, there was time to study the buds and try to determine their purpose. And, as it happens, the buds were taking the faint shape of the precursors of human limbs. Perhaps had Creature matured in a human womb, we would have seen arms and legs. But only *perhaps*.

And although Creature did actually contain some genes of immortal *HeLa* cells, human in origin, there was no quick way to determine the issue.

Colleen instinctively knew that there was a nexus somewhere along the way, yet she cognitively realised that more proof was needed. So, she encouraged Creature to allow the buds to keep developing. *Not that it had any way to stop them.*

The encouragement was necessary as Creature, when it actually became aware of the buds, also became alarmed as to what was happening to it. Colleen used all her persuasive manoeuvres to convince Creature to tolerate the buds and not try to rip them off, trying to investigate further the possible reasons for the growths.

So the mystery grew.

Matter of fact, so did Creature. By now, you could notice the change on almost a daily basis. Soon, as we have said, Frank decided he will have to devise a larger containment, and together with Colleen, he worked out and drew up the blueprints. Actually, not really *real* physical prints, but on the computer with the aid of a CAD (Computer Aided Design) program. This would be to the dimensions of the living quarters of the entity, and the dimensions eventually may be good enough to accommodate a very-very tiny child, perhaps a baby. Not that Creature was *ever* a baby.

BILL BRADBURY, CHEF INSPECTOR for the AFP was getting perplexed. In a country with a population not more than the European Union, a trio that was Colleen, Frank and Creature would at least raise some eyebrows. With the word out to all Law Agencies, someone should have been able to tweak and transmit a message to an organisation of some sort.

And because of the numerous terrorist activities in the early part of the century, all Agencies were subordinate to the Federal Police, at the apex of the pyramid. Except the Agencies which formed part of the ADF, the Australian Defence Force, who were responsible direct to the Minister for Defence.

But no, months have passed without a lead, and the Federal Minister for Defence was pressuring Bill regularly about coming up with a solution. At least a politically acceptable one.

Really, any solution, as the Honourable Minister perceived was no different to the views of other politicians on other matters. Just give me results, don't bore me with the details, or bullshit, and especially don't tell me 'why *not!*'

So the various Agencies scoured the land, and although all reasonable leads indicated a destination for the trio as Darwin, in that city itself, no further leads could be found.

Descriptions of the couple and, indeed, the trio, had been well circulated, and repeated interviews with Rail Personnel still produced no results, although the trail definitely lead north of Alice, and maybe just south of Darwin.

Of course, Bill Bradbury well realised that the group could have utilised disguises, or also branched off at any intermediate location, and then used air services as well as road, yet he had a hunch that the culprits would continue on to Darwin.

But a 'hunch' did not equate to a conviction.

Nevertheless, Darwin Local Police Command were well informed, and photographs of Colleen and Frank were distributed. Creature was also loosely introduced purportedly as a dangerous and prohibited imported animal, and its globe was unglamorously described.

It needs to be noted that naturally Colleen and Frank were clever enough to adopt disguises. Frank, who had originally sandy hair, turned into a black haired loutish-looking youth wearing heavy black-rimmed glasses, clear lenses of course, as Frank had 20-20 sight.

Colleen, who was a natural blonde, also sported black hair, cropped very short. A grungey look, although to be sure, grunge went out of fashion some 50 years ago. But they thus blended in to the fashionable, often odd, tourist scene, and they dressed accordingly. So, they looked like a pair of punky dropouts.

Frank had innumerable contacts which he accumulated over many years both in the security business and outside it. He was quite methodical to keep track of all people that have had any effect on his life, and he recorded all on his laptop and USB backup.

To be sure, Frank's laptop had far more information than the average security consultant's did. And it was a purpose-built professional machine, the fastest processor on the market, 128-bit architecture, 32 gig ram, 8 terabyte hard drive, four USB-5 ports, and the list goes on and on. Maybe it was a bit heavier than normal lap-tops, but that's the price of quality.

If one reflects on the main-frame that in the olden days Tony Haddad had (see volume I), a desk-top with Joanne Woodford at the wheel, or rather at the mouse, Frank's was more than comparable. He actually had it built to his own specifications, and it was loaded with the best software available, and then also loaded with the best security information he could gather.

But the difference between Frank and Tony Haddad was not really in technical capability, but in personal integrity and honesty. Deep down, Haddad was a scoundrel, whereas Frank was a deeply honest person. Why then did he adopt the devious trail of teaming up with Colleen?

Simply put, Frank had a basic interest in the welfare of Creature, and also of Colleen. When people are given a strong motive for some action or another, they will follow their instincts.

And Frank did just that. He wanted to be with Colleen, and with Creature.

AROUND THIS TIME, BILL BRADBURY has progressed to the position of Commissioner for the AFP, and his commitment, as well as his authority, has increased accordingly. Plus his work-load, naturally.

But in spite of his rise in and above the ranks, Bill *still* could not attain his objective; Catch Colleen and Frank, and capture Creature.

These matters were given to him as prime objectives. Regardless of anything else.

Darwin Police had a number of loose canons; people on the Territory payroll, but not really dedicated, and, sadly, willing to take payments for all sorts of illegal gains. And for acting as informers.

Darwin was a recipient destination for drugs and other illegal imports coming in from the Torres Strait and from Southeast Asia, and Indonesia, and really from all over the world.

And Darwin Harbour was leased to China. Much of this trade was via shipping containers, and the AFP had well-trained Border Force operatives to tide illegal trade.

On the other hand, the matter of Frank and Colleen was an issue well outside the scope of the Australian Border Force, and Bill was well aware of the distinction.

Just the same, he could, in his heart, feel the hangman's halter was tightening. Bits and pieces of information *were* filtering through, and when you added up the mosaics, parts of pictures were emerging.

Mind you, Bill was by now a very busy executive, and he could not capture all evidence on all matters and give it all his personal attention. But of course, he had lieutenants to do much of the ground-work.

Yet, the matter of Creature was his pet baby.

COLLEEN AND FRANK, OF course, could also feel the same trap closing. Frank had so many contacts in intelligence and general policing, that matters even seemingly irrelevant to his and Colleen's cause popped up on his computer. So, they could feel the fringes of threats encroaching on their established environment.

Frank was heavily entangled in the design and construction of larger quarters for Creature, who now had the intelligence to provide input to the design. Creature designed many aspects of his future quarters, and as who could know better than *it*, many of its suggestions have been accepted.

Like when a human designs his own home; who knows more than him what it should contain?

The finished design allowed for containment two feet two inches high, about 650 mm, and of an oval shape, with a lifting lug at the apex. Most other aspects remained the same as before. The only item of added significance was the incorporation of some lower chambers which allowed for the inclusion of accommodation for any buds that may detach from Creature. A slide-out tray could be used to capture these.

It has long before been accepted that these aberrations will happen, and Creature itself has accepted the certainty that these *would* occur. Without having a sensible cause as to their appearance on the scene.

Of the many attributes that Creature has learned to accept, there was the budding (pardon that word here) inclination to philosophy, more so acceptance of the inevitable when it arose.

The accommodation for offspring if they can be called that was a logical extension of existence, and Creature could not deny that. And these, if they eventuated, would build upon its existence on this earth.

So, the design for the new 'prison' progressed to the satisfaction of Colleen, Frank and Creature. The design was not so much a problem, but the construction may prove otherwise.

Frank's contact man in the field of acrylic construction went bankrupt, and eventually, Frank had to scout around for a dependable replacement.

So, things were getting a little tense. The actual buds on Creature could not be resolved, and so they just grew, slowly, with no solution as to their nature, or reason for them appearing.

Just another mystery to cloud the already murky waters surrounding Creature. And time passed.

FRANK WOULD USUALLY HAVE sensed any commotion around the car-park. As we know, their apartment opened onto this car-park. And usually, there was no item of excitement worth mentioning, aside of the occasional car ding or theft, and that was always well resolved by the Security or Tow-away Crews.

But this evening was different. The throng of traffic was missing. There was an eerie quietness about the place, and Frank, with his security training, knew that something was amiss.

So, he quickly conferred with Colleen, and Creature, and he called his friend, the owner of the car-park. The friend disclosed that there was a sting operation in process, and told Frank he was about to contact him about this.

That was enough for Frank. He broke out his arsenal, which was as up-to-date as any law enforcement authority would have within its grasp.

With Creature under one arm, and his all-important computer and armoury under the other, and his almost equally important mobile phone, then Colleen by his side, he led the way out into the car-park.

But not before detonating a military-grade concussion grenade in the unit, sowing confusion in the park, and to detract from the attention of any Agents probably already around the scene.

Colleen herself brought a duffle-bag, and a supply of feed and syringes for Creature, plus some scanty clothes, gathered in the space of minutes.

Frank struck out for their car, in a well-allocated spot. Having placed Creature and Colleen in the vehicle, he bolted with haste towards the outlet from the centre, clipping more than a couple of other vehicles in the rush.

During the race for the exit, two other cars joined in pursuit. These, as well, clipped more than one innocent vehicle in their path. Frank was thwarted in reaching the ground-level exit, and had to divert back to the roof-top. Why? Being a very savvy security person, he, many weeks before, parked his *other* car at the top level, of course with the authority of the Car-park's owner. His buddy.

So, whilst being chased by the unknown pursuers, he simply ditched his car at the top level, with the chasers in tow, and quick as lightning changed cars. Then driving the replacement car leisurely downwards through the many winds and turns, to the exit. 'Why leisurely?' Colleen asked. You would think he would bust his guts to get out fast, but the moderate-speed descent helped avert attention till he was actually clear.

The original path of chase continued through the car-park, and during the process, many more cars were damaged or partly destroyed. So much like the scene of various action movies involving the heroes and villains in such manoeuvres.

Back down and clear at last, they headed to the safe-house already organised by Frank long ago, just for this kind of eventuality.

The pursuers were left in a quandary until they figured out the car-switch trick. But by then, the trio were well clear of the shops, and well into the suburbs of Darwin.

In the safe house, they recovered themselves. Clean up, feed Creature, call the airport for a booking, all went like a well-oiled machine. Frank was certainly an expert in these manoeuvres.

They were fortunate to get a booking by Jetstar to Brisbane, and Frank, from Darwin airport, contacted a number of his seemingly inexhaustible army of buddies.

After an uneventful although bumpy flight, upon landing at Brisbane, and passing through Customs, they soon found themselves in a cab, ushered in by the driver on sight. Screeching off the kerbside, they were driven through the suburbs to Inala, a Brisbane suburb, peopled by all races including many Aborigines.

It seemed as though they were expected. Colleen thought maybe it had something to do with Frank's phone call from Darwin Airport, but she didn't question it. She just accepted it.

The cab took them through many areas taking tortuous turns here and there, and in the end Colleen was totally lost. She didn't really know Brisbane at all.

The driver and Frank did not converse, after Frank gave him some terse instructions at the start.

They pulled up in front of a Federation brick house, in a quiet street, lined with huge fig trees. The blinds in the front window fluttered a little, obviously with someone observing their arrival.

Then they got out of the cab, and Colleen noted that no payment took place. Everything was taken up onto the old-fashioned ceramic tiled patterned- floor veranda, then the front door opened and they were faced by a young man wearing a turtle-neck sweater.

He urged them inside, and Colleen observed that the two men embraced like brothers may. The gear including Creature in his sphere were speedily taken inside, and within seconds, no sign of their arrival could be detected.

From the outside, that is; inside was another story. Freshly made coffee and toast soon gave up their aroma, and after introductions they all sat around the table in the really old-fashioned house. Very high ceilings, tiles instead of skirting boards and picture rails on every wall. Even stained-glass fronts to the kitchen cupboards.

The young man's name was Gavin Hoffman, and he offered the toast commenting; 'raisin toast. Okay with you, Colleen?' And she responded; 'sure, one of my favourites.'

Some small talk, and then Frank elaborated to Colleen on Gavin, explaining that he was an SAS (Special Air Service Regiment) soldier, part of the Special Covert Operations Command, in active service, but on call. That is, he could continue living at his house instead of the barracks, but 'at the ready' 24/7.

Additionally, he had to attend full time two days and nights at the barracks. Frank explained that they were old friends, and have served together in Europe and the Middle East, in days long gone.

After feeding, Creature was formally introduced to Gavin, who had a little trouble getting his head around the whole concept, but in the spirit of the SAS motto ('He Who Dares Wins') he soon adapted to the challenge. As a matter of fact, Gavin and Creature soon begun to chat -so to speak.

It was explained by Frank for the benefit of Colleen and Creature that Gavin was member of a network of soldiers who were constantly on call both in matters of National Security and also on other matters not usually in the public eye.

Such as being part of the Special Covert Operations Command.

The little foursome soon turned into a bit of a party, as the participants soon accepted each other as valued comrades.

The three 'humans' imbued some wine, but as for Creature, this was one threshold that may or may not eventually have to be crossed. For now, an injection of nutrients administered by Colleen was sufficient, and although this cannot be compared to a nice *drop*, Creature was happy enough. Or at least it seemed to be. Evidenced by the lack of angry emanations.

Gavin allocated a fairly large family room for the group, with an on-suite attached. It would do until a more suitable place could be found, preferably another safe-house, but with enough room to establish a laboratory.

In the interim, they opened their scant luggage and placed the items into the built-in wardrobe that also adorned their room. Frank's weaponry found a home next door to that owned by Gavin, also in that room, except the pistol which, having regard for the recent events, Frank decided to keep under his pillow. Full time.

It may be a good time now to touch on the subject of how Frank managed to get his arsenal through the security gates at both Darwin and Brisbane.

Well, some more of his 'buddies' came into the scene, employed at Airport Security. It would be amazing to the average person to realise just how much of these sorts of activities goes on under the noses of Management, and pass undetected. Of course, not cabin baggage.

Before turning in, Frank elaborated a little on his earlier relationship with Gavin. This started in Germany during the tail-off of the Muslim Wars, and many Europeans were recruited and trained there, then shipped to all corners of the Middle East.

Frank and Gavin spent periods of time in the Levant, Iraq, Kuwait and the United Arab Emirates.

They were in the same platoon, when on an occasion of conflict at Umm Qasr in Iraq, near Kuwait.

Frank was pleased for his posting there as his hobby was archaeology and **Alexander the Great** supposedly made his landing at Umm Qasr in 325 BC.

Frank was at the time Corporal, and Gavin was Private First Class. The Platoon Commander, a Lieutenant, was killed in action, but his body was not released by the Iraqi Islamist insurgents. It was the job of Frank's squad to recover the body for despatch to the lieutenant's family in Belgium. At the moment, it was held for ransom.

Normally, the squad would have been led by a Sergeant, but manpower restrictions meant that the next senior in rank would lead the assault.

And that was Corpora Frank Vagyoczki.

The operation began this day at 00.00 Zulu time, and Frank, Gavin and eight more troopers made a stealth approach towards the enemy's stronghold.

As they were creeping forward, in a line, at a certain time their cover was blown by an Iraqi forward sentry, who opened gunfire with what sounded like an ancient Kalashnikov AK47. Gavin was hit in the left knee, and fell immediately.

The initial shot opened up the whole front, with firing from both sides. Frank made the decision to abort the mission, and gave the signal for retreat.

As Gavin had only one leg to stand on, and was in severe pain, Frank hoisted him up on his shoulders, and staggered back to the friendly lines, where Gavin was extracted by helicopter and flown to Kuwait City.

Gavin had knee replacement surgery, and Frank was decorated for bravery under fire.

About this last statement; Frank did not disclose to Colleen the fact about this, as he did not want to appear a braggart. He just told her that he was praised for his effort.

The Lieutenant's body was never recovered.

So, that was the story of the start of Frank and Gavin's friendship.

About the quarters at Gavin's house; not bad for the first night away from 'home.' Still, the strange environment was a little disturbing, you get so used to the tiniest noises in your normal environment; those same noises in a different lodging sound exaggerated. And of course, there are some new ones.

Halfway into the night, it was Frank that detected a strange sound, and he immediately woke fully, and due to his training, he was totally alert in a second. Eyes wide open. He nudged Colleen, and whispered into her ear; 'wake up but be quiet. Something is not right.' Colleen also awoke immediately, and they were both alert and still.

Tinkle.

The sound was subdued, but unmistakably glass-on-glass, or glass-on-a-hard-surface. It came from the direction of the sideboard, where Creature was placed for the time being.

The pair strained their eyes, but nothing could be seen, and also strained their ears, which soon detected another 'tinkle.'

Frank whispered; 'you stay here' to Colleen, as he crept out of the bed, and slowly moved towards the sideboard. Gun in one hand. Torch in the other. In the dark, he allowed his toes to find their way to the edge of the carpet, then with one sweep of his arms he cocked the gun in one hand, and simultaneously clicked on the torch with the other.

He did not know what he expected but he froze at the sight that greeted his eyes.

CREATURE WAS IN HIS sphere, but instead of hanging by his vertices as was usual, he was lying flat on top of the upper shelf.

Outside the sphere was an empty wine bottle, no cork, the one they opened last night, but left with maybe 10% before being finally corked. The bottle was then left on the kitchen table, as was the hypodermic syringe and needle that Colleen had used to feed Creature in the evening.

Frank noted that the syringe was now on the sideboard, before being startled by a touch on his shoulder.

It was Colleen, who also silently crept out of the bed and was right behind Frank. 'What is happening,' she whispered to him when he said, in normal speech, that she may as well just flick the light on.

He laid the gun and torch on the sideboard, and stared at Creature in amazement. Colleen said; 'why is it laying down instead of being suspended?'

Frank could hardly contain himself, then he just started laughing.

'Creature is *pissed*, or should I say politely *drunk*,' he finally said.

Obviously, it used psychokinesis and psycho-levitation to open the bedroom door, then move the bottle with the little bit of wine into the bedroom, then the same with the syringe. It then opened the bottle, laid it on its side, inserted the needle and drew out some wine. Then it thrust the needle through the membrane on the port on his sphere, and squirted the wine into this.

'I don't believe it,' said Colleen.

'See for yourself,' said Frank, still laughing.

And sure enough, Creature gave all the appearance of a drunk living being. 'It may be sick,' she said to Frank.

Frank said. 'Colleen, face facts. It is simply *pissed*. And he continued laughing.'

'But how? Why?'

'Well, it saw us having a drink, a few laughs, generally a good time. So it thought; *why not me?*'

Creature just lay there for a while longer, then, with the creeping movements of an octopus, it climbed back into its usual stance. Vertical. But wobblily so.

Colleen said; 'I just cannot accept all this.'

And Frank said; 'I cannot, either.'

The two stared into each other's eyes, in disbelief.

Colleen said; 'Creature, can you explain what happened here?'

The response was not what she expected. The emanation from Creature simply said;

*'It's **my** business.'*

A knock on the door. Gavin, in a low voice; 'is everything okay in there?' Frank replied that all was well.

Gavin revealed that he heard some tinkling, got up, and then noticed the light of the torch under the door. He said he was just making sure all was okay.

Would Frank open the door so Gavin can be sure all *is* well.

Frank said, in low key to Colleen; 'something is not right here.'

Colleen; 'I am already packing. Then to Creature; 'Creature, make no noise.'

Then all hell broke loose. Front door being broken down with a door-ram, windows smashed, then hammering on their door; 'open up in there.'

Then Gavin's voice; 'Frank, you better do as they demand.'

During the last minutes, Colleen was hastily packing their essentials, whilst Frank was busy checking his arsenal.

Then Frank; 'Gav, what is going on?' And all the while still getting his gear ready. Gavin responded; 'Frank, it's no good. Please open the door or it will be broken down.'

Frank said; 'give us a moment to get dressed decent.

But in the interim, what is happening?'

Gavin, in a tense voice; 'Frank, you and I learned the value of *delaying tactics* long ago, and together. Please, don't stall, just open up.'

Frank; 'just one moment. Colleen is stark naked.

Then to Colleen; 'insert your ear plugs.' Colleen did that, she was always carrying the plugs ready for use since the early days in Darwin, when Frank instructed her in some of the intricacies of covert operations.

And with that, he opened the door a crack and threw a standard-issue M-84 live stun-grenade through the gap.

Colleen to Creature; 'quiet, please.' And grabbed the container along with her scantily-packed suitcase.

Then she stood ready waiting for Frank's order.

Frank, embroiled in memories of past comradeship, thinking about his rescue of Gavin, stood bitterly for one split moment. Then, survival instinct replaced the temporary loss of combative ability. Frank became the potential killing machine as he was trained to be.

The SAS team in the entry to the house were caught by surprise, as the grenade exploded. Frank was known to be a capable agent in the olden days, but he was not known to be equipped with weaponry, such as the M-84's.

In the confusion, Frank and Colleen, carrying Creature, were in train to evacuate the house. Frank chose a rear-fence exit, and although SAS commandos controlled doors and most windows, our heroes managed to reach the rear fence, climb over, and escape into the darkness.

Snaking between bushes, trees and other obstacles, and over fences they also managed to sight a metal garden shed some four properties away from their original scene.

This, they entered.

Just in time, as helicopters swarmed over the night sky, and trained their laser-guided spotter-lights all over the ground below.

But in this smallish galvanised-iron enclosure, Colleen and Frank found their refuge – for the moment.

This gave Frank enough time to again sort out his weaponry, which he did with great, almost obsessive, care.

But then the foot-soldiers of the SAS team swept the neighbourhood. In not a lot of time, they found the refugees.

And the stand-off continued.

The escapees inside the tin shed. The SAS personnel on the outside.

Frank was once again checking his armoury.

With a worried look on her face, Colleen said; 'Frank, surely you are not going to use these weapons?'

'Only to confuse, not hurt, the raiders. I don't intend any loss of life' said Frank

'But what if they fire on you? Will you return the fire?'

'In *tha*t case, only to wound, to stop them.'

'And grenades? What about them, if you use them?'

'I only have stun grenades.'

Then Creature emanated; 'open the door, Frank, and put me on the threshold.'

Frank said; 'Creature, are you crazy? We've done all this to keep you from being captured.'

Creature emanated; 'Frank, do what I *tell* you.' This time the tone changed. Creature was now giving *orders!*

Frank looked at Colleen. Colleen said; 'It has certain abilities, Frank. Let' try. The situation is hopeless, anyhow.'

Frank said; 'right.' And he shouted to the outside; 'hold your fire. I am opening the door.'

And he did. He put the globe right on the threshold.

Three of the commandos were at the door. Others were hidden from sight, but were dispersed around the garden. Two choppers still hovered overhead.

And then the commandos got a surprise.

Without commotion, all their weapons were wrenched out of their hands. And pistols from their holsters. As if blown by some wind, or an unseen force, all the weapons flew away from the troops, over the trees, the rooftops.

The commandos stared in disbelief. And Frank and Colleen, taking advantage of the confusion and carrying the sphere, ran down the side lane, out to the street. The next crossroads were a main road, and they headed there.

Colleen recalled Creature's performance in disarming Jim Mullens, and later Joe Kadas, in times past (ONCO III). This was the same scenario.

Once clear of Gavin's area, they tried to hail a cab, and after two unsuccessful attempts, they finally got one. Where to?

Frank had one more address. Through the rear window, they could see the commotion starting up at the corner. But by that time, they were more than two blocks away, and Frank gave the destination to the driver, this being a block away from the *real* address, in Brisbane's Fortitude Valley, often just referred to as 'The Valley.'.

To be dropped just a block away was only to reduce the risk of tracking.

When they alighted from the cab, they had maybe 200 metres to walk.

Frank was talking on his mobile to his friend Brett Snellman during most of the taxi trip, and he told Colleen that Brett was home and would be waiting. He explained to Colleen that this was his last contact in Brisbane that he felt he could trust.

'Like you did Gavin?' Colleen could not stop herself from making this comment, and then she bit her lip and said to Frank, 'I am sorry. I am just *so* tense.'

And Frank responded, 'I know just what you mean. And I am disappointed in Gavin for selling us out, but we must remember it was *his job* that he was doing, and in his game, personalities sometimes must be pushed into the background. And Gavin, being the patriot that all Special Services troops are, *had* to do what he did.'

Brett Snellman was a handsome looking young man, tall, athletic, strong features, curly black hair and *incredibly* bright blue eyes, and Colleen found him likeable from the start. He was also a Special Forces commando, but he was living on-base, not like Gavin. It so happened that this was his day off, ad Frank was grateful for *that*. Brett was basically living with his mother Melissa, who was away at this time.

He and Frank had a long talk, with Colleen present, and all cards were laid on the table. When Brett excused himself for a toilet break, Colleen whispered to Frank, 'Frank, you are giving away an awful lot. Is that wise?'

Frank was not in the right mood to field questions, but he understood Colleen's concern. So he curbed his sensitiveness to the topic, and assured Colleen that Brett was more trustworthy than Gavin, whereupon Colleen said, 'so then why did you pick Gavin first?

Frank simply said, 'well, we were in an emergency situation starting from Darwin. Beggars can't be choosers, we had to have someone, and Gavin was more readily available. He was at home, whereas Brett was at that time at the Base.'

'Mind you, I did not expect Gav to betray us. But I guess in hindsight I could have foreseen it. Only to Gavin, this would not seem like betrayal. He would have weighed up our personal friendship against his duty. I guess duty won out.'

'What about Brett?'

'He is a closer friend than Gavin. But apart from that, he is in a less senior position than Gavin. In fact, Gavin is his boss, so to speak. So Brett would be less likely to heed the call of duty.

But there are no guarantees in life, especially in the Special Services game. So, we just have to see what develops.'

Colleen was less convinced. But the options were running out.

She had no choice but to agree.

CREATURE REMAINED SILENT DURING all this. But at a certain time, it emanated; 'Colleen, I won't think less of you if you give me up. I don't want you to endanger yourself any further. And besides, I have all these buds growing out of me, and you have not determined what they are. What does the future hold, anyhow?'

'Creature, I know how hard it is for you. After all, you are in the centre of all this. But I am not ready to give you up, and I know Frank feels the same. As for the buds, we really have no real idea, other than they may just possibly be your offspring. How do you feel about that idea?'

'It feels horrendous to me.'

'Creature, have you considered that like everything else in this world, you may have come into being for a purpose? Perhaps a very special one?'

'Yes, Colleen, I have. And I also have read many of your books, and of course, used the internet. Many subjects I have read about include Creationism, Evolutionism, Cosmogonical views and Theology, plus Eschatology. And many other subjects, including Philosophy.'

'I go along with your thoughts that I *may* have come into being for a purpose. But no matter where I look or how hard I try, there is no purpose for my being here *that I can find*.

It seems to me that I always return to the same plea. *Please, Colleen, help me. I am afraid!'*

Colleen was staring out the window of the unit at the hustle-bustle that is Brisbane City. And she had no ready answers any more than she did at earlier times. So much had happened in only a few days. The lodgings at Darwin were so wonderful. *And* private.

Then, she could carry out experiments, observe Creature at her leisure, and she always had Frank as a sounding board. And, she recorded all matters of relevance on a small digital recorder that Frank had bought her. 64 gigabytes, you could almost store a library on it.

Unfortunately, since they absconded from Darwin, there was not a moment for reflections of any kind. Survival took the front of the stage.

But Creature's buds were growing. Slowly, but certainly. As Margaret Wheatley put it at the meeting that seemed so long ago, the genus Hydra, phylum cnidaria, (who in the world dreams up these taxonomical definitions?) produced such buds as a means of procreation. Then again, Creature certainly contained some of the genes from the human *HeLa* cells, which are truly immortal.

Can the reader follow Colleen's thoughts, where for a moment, she allowed her mind to stray to the plight of Henrietta Lacks, an African-American girl who was made pregnant by her first cousin at age 13 and from whose cervix the so-called *HeLa* cancer cells were harvested without her knowledge or consent. These then provided the immortal cell-line, which was (and still is at he time of writing these works) viable the best part of a century after Henrietta herself died in 1951.

Colleen continued musing; so what combination of these factors were at play in Creature, and the whole thing may conceivably had nothing to do with this baffling entity. Maybe, it all was a completely unknown and almost unimaginable phenomenon.

She said to Creature; 'I know you are afraid. I would be, too. But have heart, Creature. We are trying for you.

And I feel for you – I really do.'

THE TACTICAL RESPONSE UNIT of the Australian Federal Police were not sitting on their hands. The Federal Ministers for National Security and also Defence made sure that all the wheels kept turning, and were well oiled.

The unit included the Special Forces Command, who were rapped over the knuckles about the Darwin fiasco, and the one at Brisbane not much later. The seeming ease with which Colleen and Frank evaded capture did not sit well in Canberra.

Bill Bradbury was recently promoted to Commissioner of the AFP, the Australian Federal Police. And since he knew both Colleen and Frank from way back, and since he had also encountered Creature, there was no other person more suited to lead the attempts to capture the trio.

Bill had at his disposal the head of ASIO, the Australian Security Intelligence Organisation, and also the Signals Directorate, represented by General Robert Menzies, at the Situation Room in Canberra, who latter was very involved in the matter of Creature. He initiated the abortive raid at Darwin.

Therefore, Menzies was eminently suited to endeavours to attempt to recover his reputation which diminished somewhat in the failure of the Darwin raid.

Bill Bradbury was also stung by the same failure. He committed himself and his associates to the task of bringing this matter to end.

And in the National Security framework, many questions arose. The possible destination of the trio, the purpose of their separation from the Weapons Development Authority, the seemingly clear escape from the net of Internal Security.…..all of this came into play.

Paul Mitchell also did not escape some criticism, as his establishment was the scene of departure of the fugitives. After Woomera/Maralinga, National Security had no clues until the afore-mentioned raid at Darwin, which was somewhat less than fruitful.

Then came Brisbane, also less than successful, in spite of the betrayal by Gavin.

Now, hopefully safe in the home of Brett, things could not settle down, as the events at Gavin's house placed the trio fairly in the cross-hairs at Brisbane. The Government threw added resources into the effort at that City, and the noose was once *again* tightening, so to speak.

Gavin did not know of the connection between Frank and Brett; had he known, the next step could have been a raid on Brett's home.

But, lucky for our heroes, Gavin was not yet aware of the latter's friendship with Frank. Gavin and Frank went back to Europe and Iraq. Brett, on the other hand, struck up with Frank in Afghanistan; a different Command, a different theatre of operations.

Frank thus became the fulcrum between Gavin and Brett, and he was careful not to give Brett any indication about the trio's location the previous night.

Nevertheless, the Government Agencies were not fools, and Frank was aware that eventually the trails would cross. So, it was important to use every minute in locating a safe house away from Brett, too.

COLLEEN AND FRANK BECAME aware of a sudden onslaught of emanations of pain from Creature. It was about midday, and they were munching on some takeaway food that Frank brought in a few minutes before.

Frank said, 'what the hell, Creature?'

And the latter emanated, 'get these horrible bugs out of here!'

'Bugs? What bugs? Nothing can get into your sphere, unless we consider the sprayed-in nourishment, as intrusion. So what the *hell* are you talking about, Creature?'

'Can't you see, Frank? They're all over me!' And Creature started uncontrollably shivering, whilst emanating feelings of panic.

The objects of fear turned out to be not panic-worthy, but certainly astonishing. They were the lumps.

Creature was having babies. Well, not in the conventional sense, perhaps. Not as we are accustomed to. But as Creature shivered, Colleen and Frank could see small particles falling off it. These appeared to correspond to the 'buds' already observed on Creature, which in turn appeared to be similar to the ones seen on Hans, a long time ago.

But never have they been observed in a free state. Only embedded under the skin, in the case of Hans, and under the membrane, which seemed to coat Creature.

In the current event, the particles dropped onto the floor of the sphere. Or rather, the special removable bottom shelf. And the 'shivering' was an automatic reaction of living things to irritation, much like a dog shivers or shakes himself to be rid of parasites like fleas, or, of course, just water, or dust.

So there it was. Instead of coping with one creature, now Colleen and Frank had maybe a dozen. And Creature itself hated having them around. They frightened him. Any analogy to other living things? Colleen and Frank could not think of any. Most living things actually protect their young. Others may just leave them alone to hatch from eggs without further interaction, like turtles, just for example.

And while our heroes were pondering over such things, Creature emitted 'I am hungry.'

Much like a woman might say after the stress of child-birth. Food of course helps the body to recuperate.

Colleen said, 'if we feed Creature, won't that also feed the buds?'

Still, she gave Creature a shot of nutrient.

Frank; 'what choice do we have?' To Creature; 'What do you want?'

Creature emitted, 'I told you already, get these monstrosities out of my sphere.'

Frank was perplexed. 'If we get them out, what shall we do with them? Kill them?'

Colleen interjected; 'those things need to be destroyed. They would be vectors of highly infectious cancer. The same as Creature.'

'Frank to Creature; 'you heard all this. What do you think?'

Creature emitted; 'kill them.' Frank was getting rattled, 'how do you propose we do that?' Creature responded, 'incinerate them. You humans are good at that.' Referring no doubt to the Hans episode, back in time.

'Your *own* offspring?' Said a horrified Frank.

Colleen said to Frank, 'those issues should not concern us. Those things are just tiny blobs of tissue. Let's not use terms like 'offspring.' Frank, I already said, they are vectors of unbelievable and vicious disease. Let's get to work.'

A moment's pause. Then action.

Frank withdrew a baking tray from the wall oven. Then he told Colleen to bring out her mini hair-spray. Putting the tray on top of the oven, he readied a long barbecue match Brett had in the kitchen drawer.

He then withdrew the bottom tray of Creature's enclosure, and tipped the contents onto the baking tray. These were like tiny pieces of dog-biscuit, by appearance. Or in more Australian idiom, like Weet-Bix which is a breakfast cereal.

Then he told Colleen to start spraying them from her hair-spray, which she did, and whilst the mist hung over the buds, Frank lighted a match, and held it into the stream of spray. Instantly, the spray turned to flame, setting the buds to fire.

She emptied the whole can, and then almost all that was left on the tray were charred pieces, slowly smouldering. However, there were a few pieces scorched but otherwise unburned, and Frank was not satisfied with this.

He foraged around the kitchen drawers, and found some alfoil baking bags. So Colleen slid all the remains into one of these bags, then folded the bag and put it all into another bag. Finally satisfied, Colleen sealed this last bag with the special tape provided.

Frank said, 'we will have these remnants scientifically examined, when we can get our heads above water. In the meantime, they can stay with us along with Creature.

Creature had stopped shivering, and hung in its usual configuration. It seemed relieved. Then it emanated; 'Frank, they were *not* my offspring.

They were tumours on my body. If I did not get rid of them, they would have attacked me.

Frank said, 'tumours upon a tumour?' Then; 'no offence.'

Creature emanated, 'so to speak.'

THE MINISTER FOR DEFENCE was getting to the next step after impatience. He called a meeting at Canberra, with Paul Mitchell, Robert Menzies, Bill Bradbury, Jim Mullens and one or some others and hauled them over the coals.

He started by letting forth a bellicose tirade where he let them all know how he felt. Amongst other things, he wanted to know how it was possible that in a nation boasting the best intelligence community, the envy of all western countries, organisations still could not produce enough skill to capture a trio including only two humans and a small entity that the best brains have been unable to identify.

He said, 'you had them in your hands (referring to the raid at Gavin Hoffman's place) and then they were gone. And the best of Special Operations Executives, on whose training and sustenance the Government forks out an inordinately indecent amount annually, with egg all over their faces. And over mine, too, according to the Prime Minister.'

'I ask you, gentlemen, what possible excuse can you all create for this abject failure, and the further failure to, since that day, not turn up a single cue?'

He went on, 'Jim, close the doors.' Then; 'I am going to drop the polite bullshit. I want fucking results, and I want them *now*. I can find new heads for each and all of your Departments. Unless you resolve this disgrace without further delay, your fucking jobs hang just by a thread.'

Now, the Minister was not prone to profanity just for the sake of it. The manner in with he spoke was just an indication of the fury he felt, and all present realised this.

The Minister finished up. 'From tomorrow, I want a report of each day's activities by each of you on my desk. *Every day*. Goodbye, gentlemen.'

The fact that he added the word 'gentlemen' to his tirade was not lost by any of the attendees. It meant that the Minister still had regard for every one of them, although the extent of his regard was certainly less than it had ever been previously.

Bill Bradbury lost no time. The moment the group was out the door, he was on the cell phone to his most senior aide, Allen Neich. Allen happened to be half-brother to Brett Snellman, although this fact has no relevance to our tale. His orders to Allen were; 'pull every available Agent from all assignments and build a task-group to catch Colleen, Frank and Creature.

Allen, no excuses will be accepted. This matter must come to a conclusion. I will see you in Canberra, before I head for Adelaide.'

FRANK SAID TO COLLEEN; 'I cannot get my head around Creature and the buds that fell off it. Something is just not right, here.

It's almost like a human mother killing her own babies. And I don't buy that Creature thought that the buds would attack it.'

Colleen; 'Creature was genuine in its fear. What about that?'

Frank said, 'just as we- humanity - have created a monster unwittingly, and then the monster reared its head in Hans, perhaps Creature has allowed these buds to grow within its body, then later to realise they were monsters *to it.*'

Colleen pondered on this for a while. Then she said; 'I'm not really inclined to agree with you. But then, what to do with Creature? It is a loose cannon in our world. And then, what about the Onco food production line? Is that more dangerous than we thought?'

BRIAN ARCHWALD HAD PROBLEMS. In the euphoria after his receipt of the Nobel Prize, all looked rosy.

But some disturbing factors arose in time. At a certain point, one of the supposedly irradiated packages of Onco product, given to a part

Aboriginal Australian, became the prime reason - so it was speculated - for that individual to contract cancer.

It came out that during the irradiation of the product before packaging there was a short power failure at the Facility.

It was discovered that during the short period of lack of irradiation, Onco cells multiplied in an unexpected way, and at an unexpected speed.

The aboriginal individual died in a fashion reminiscent of the Hans episode. Except no flames. And he was buried in ancestral land in the New Guinea Highlands, Chimbu Province, near Mt. Hagen, where he originally came from, the return on request by his relatives.

Then, soon, there was an outbreak of Kuru in the area.

Kuru is related to 'mad cow disease' and also to 'scrapie' in sheep, and is caused by misfolded prion protein molecules in the brain of an affected person or other being.

These misfolded proteins when in contact with normal ones, cause the latter to misfold also, and infect other proteins. The whole process becomes like a chain reaction.

Transmission is via the ancestral ritualistic custom of relatives eating from the brains of dead affected persons. In doing so, they imagine they take on the powers of wisdom and strength of their ancestors.

It eventually turned out that the aboriginal was of the Fore tribe, some having migrated to Australia a while ago, and that on return of the body to Papua New Guinea, relatives partook of the remains in accordance with ancient customs and rituals.

It seemed likely that the prion protein in the brain of this individual interacted with Onco particles, causing the proliferation of the disease. Brian was concerned about the prospect of a new global pandemic.

He had been in periodical communication with Colleen and Frank over time, bypassing all formal channels. Brian's interest was basically in Creature, enhanced by the death of Hans. Colleen and Frank of course had an interest in the Onco Production Line, and its effect on Creature.

Brian told Frank; 'this thing is getting out of all control. What we originally thought was a panacea for planetary life, is now heading for a pandemic instead.

Frank, you have to *kill* Creature. It is the probable source of future endemics, although not kuru, along with the Onco product. Cannot stop *that* production, although we have installed an UPS (Uninterruptible Power Supply) to avoid repeating past mistakes. So no further outages.'

'But we cannot allow things to go any further. And I know that you and Colleen have developed an affection for Creature which is a bit bizarre, to be blunt about it. But emotions have no place in a major threat to the human race. You and Colleen just *have* to terminate it.'

Here, dear reader, we will mention that Brian had no business to meddle in a matter hotly pursued by the authorities. But, then, Brian was Brian, not the most conventional person by any means. Yet he was loyal to his staff and even ex-staff, more loyal than to the Government.

He did not know where the fugitive trio were residing at. Frank sporadically called Brian, and did not reveal his location. So all conversations were initiated by Frank. Security, you know.

Frank finally said to Brian, 'I will talk it over with Colleen.'

And so he did. At a time he considered appropriate, he said to Colleen, 'Honey, sit with me for a while and let's talk about Creature.

Colleen said, 'What's the new problem, Frank?'

They were sitting in the lounge, filled with a range of indoor plants. Brett and his mother Melissa loved greenery.

Colleen had been, just a few minutes before, talking with Judy Hewitt; she still kept up the contact with both her and Natasha Stott (ONCO III); well, a girl had to have some social contact besides the rigorous entanglement with matters connected with Creature, and more mundane house-keeping chores, although the style of life her and Frank adopted did not really need much of *that*.

Judy wanted to know how she was, how it was going with Frank, and how Creature was faring, whilst still on the run. She also asked Colleen was she happy? To which Colleen responded with 'as happy as one can be, considering the circumstances.'

Colleen never gave away her location at any one time, and since she has changed her mobile number, Judy could not call her. Colleen did all the calling.

Similar to Frank calling Brian occasionally.

Frank really hated to upset Colleen, over the past many months he had grown genuinely fond of her. And she of him.

Frank said, 'Brian has been in my ear,' and he related all that Brian told him, including the 'kuru' incident. And Brian's request to kill Creature. Whereupon Colleen became horrified, and told Frank so.

She virtually brought Creature up from a 'mongrel dog,' as Jim Mullens had put it long ago, to an intelligent and articulate being, if somewhat weird.

'What does Brian think,' she said, 'does he think of it as some kind of alien?' Then she bit her lip. That fact of the matter was that Creature was more like an alien than anything else.

'Oh hell,' she said." Who am I kidding? We cannot fight the whole Government. One day, Creature will be captured, along with us. And then what? And in the interim, what battles will we have to fight? And for what?'

Just then, the sound of breaking glass, and simultaneously of breaking plywood.

Frank reached for his pistol, but laying her hand on his, Colleen said, 'No, Frank. No killing.'

And then the house was filled with commandos. They entered simultaneously through windows, and also the front door, and the door to the room the couple were in.

The leader of the attack team said, tersely, to Frank; 'Where is the fugitive?' Referring, of course, to Creature. Frank paused, then nodded towards the family room, connected to the lounge.

'Hands behind your back, you two.' One of his offsiders clamped handcuffs on wrists, whilst removing Frank's weapon.

The team leader moved into the family room, where Creature was sitting, or rather hanging, in its globe, on the table.

He then removed a flame syringe from his kit-bag. Then to the sphere, and without hesitation he injected a flammable accelerant fluid into the porthole in the sphere. Then, he injected a fire initiator compound and with the press of a button, ignited it.

All this in a sequence within seconds between each action.

Then, Creature, although caught unawares, unleashed its formidable defence mechanism in no time, and the accelerant stream stopped in an instant, whilst the ignitative also immediately stopped its flammable action.

Creature hung in its usual place barely scorched, and then a series of emissions eventuated. The first, a psychokinetic one removed all weapons from the attackers. The second barricaded, although incompletely, all physical contact between them and the family room.

The third was a distress call to Frank and to Colleen, both of whom received and understood the call, but were unable to respond.

But the raiders were not disabled.

The fall-back position was to initiate an emission of a poisonous gas, directed straight into the sphere via a specific-purpose nozzle. Having done this, the commandos, by now wearing breathing apparatus, retreated to a holding position.

During this time, Colleen and Frank were evacuated via a waiting chopper. Then to Amberley Air Base, then by a waiting Lear jet aircraft to Canberra. Also at this time, Brett arrived back from the Base, and was completely surprised by the events unfolding at his home.

He was handed a gas mask on arrival, which he donned.

The poisonous gas did its job. Creature had no defence against this, and within moments, it succumbed to the fumes.

The most formidable adversary the human race has ever seen, writhing in agony, still hanging on by its vertices, then it died.

Or did it?

Colleen and Frank were whisked away in the first chopper. Brett followed in another. The Team Leader, clutching the now-deceased (?) Creature in its sphere, followed in still another helicopter, together with his men.

When the Minister for Defence laid his cards on the table some time earlier, he was not fooling around.

Assets such as three helicopters in one sequence plus a Lear jet would not be sourced except in response to dire matters. Such as mass-terrorism.

But the Defence Department's seriousness was amply displayed by the application of resources, human and machine, deployed in this scene.

The end of all these events, we could hardly have contemplated. *But all things do come to an end.*

Don't they?

The End.
(but is there more to follow?)

Actually, there *is*.

On arrival at Canberra, all previous participants were de-briefed.

ASIS, the Australian Secret Intelligence Service, provided well-trained operatives and executives to the Project.

All participants were vetted, and all information gained was processed through the data bank that was the heart of ASIS.

And, as may be expected, people that had any part in the Onco adventure, wanted to set eyes on the centre of all the attention.

CREATURE WAS BROUGHT IN to the central laboratory at Canberra. Still in its sphere, it appeared limp and truly dead. Various scientists mulled around it's remains, and some tests were carried out, like X-rays, ultrasounds, and MRI, and other non-intrusive procedures.

The fact is, no-one wanted to touch the thing, or get too close to it.

It was decided that the entity should not be removed from its sphere until all safety procedures were first installed and working.

And until a defence against its mental manipulations could be found, just in case.

In the interim, Creature, entombed in its sphere, was placed in a refrigerated compartment in the morgue being part of the ASIS -ASIO facility.

During the next shift at the morgue, the Forensic Examiner experienced a strange and disturbing event.

The drawer housing Creature opened inexplicably by itself, leaving Creature sitting in the open drawer, in its sphere, seemingly waiting for something to happen.

But it was dead, was it not?

The Examiner alerted the Control Room, and waited for instructions. Then the emanation, from the direction of the drawer; 'open the special port; I need air.'

The Examiner was not at all prepared for this; usually, the contents of the drawers were cadavers awaiting autopsy, and certainly none of the inhabitants had ever opened their drawers. *Let alone try for conversation.*

Next, the emanation; 'come and open my prison (the enclosure) and let me out.'

The Examiner was just a basic medical officer, not at all trained in such events or anything like it, and to him, the most obvious act was to do as he was asked. Especially as Creature has long ago learned to add a commanding tone to its emissions......when it so chose.

The Examiner, by opening the 'Third Port' in the sphere, possibly released on the world potentially the most deadly plague it had ever experienced. And when later examined by his superiors, he had no recollection of the event. And a little after this, he died. Highly invasive Cancer.

IN ITS ENTIRE LIFE, Creature was, for the first time, free of restrictions.

And for the first time ever, it was free of its prison, the globe. Creature had, throughout its imprisonment, evolved.

Soon, Judy and Colleen would not have recognised it.

And when the Examiner allowed it freedom, it was a heady experience for it. Never before could it experience the world first hand, away from the restraints of its sphere. How?

What has happened was that the gas intended to kill it only resulted in its being dazed, anaesthetised, and when the effects wore off, it was as functional as before.

So, now, there was Creature free from any restraints. Open to the world, and *this* being open to it.

Was it ready? Or was the world ready?

And what about its 'offspring,' so to speak?

FRANK AND COLLEEN WERE placed before a tribunal. Separate hearings, of course, but the same charges.

The charges were expropriation of Government property, then of dereliction of duty, then causing commotion, then of civil damages during the flight of the escapees from the car-park, then Gavin's home, the list went on and on.

The charges of course were a mixture of criminal and civil features. Lawyers had to untangle the matters and cases were built accordingly.

The result was the judgement by the magistrates in each case, suitably prompted by the Government Prosecutor, which was to drop all charges, due to the obvious lack of precedent in case law.

Colleen and Frank were thus freed from all punitive action, and, in fact, were not taken off the Government payroll.

The Government, being desperate for expert people to handle the Onco fiasco, tacitly agreed with the judgements.

BUT WHAT ABOUT CREATURE? And the World?

Yes, what about all that?

CREATURE JUST SAT -INAPPROPRIATE word, as not having a rear end, it could not of course *sit, per se.* However, lacking the appropriate word in English, we will just settle for 'sat.'

That is, it sat in the open morgue drawer, until it could fully (more or less) appreciate its new-found freedom.

And the fact that it did not feel to be in any danger, which was a most heady concept, as all its life it had been enclosed, and so protected, by an acrylic sphere. All feeding and enabled breathing and other needs of life having been provided by humans. Especially Judy and Colleen. And Frank.

So, Creature sat in the open morgue drawer, contemplating 'what next?'

It had no problem being surrounded by cadavers. Being of different substance to them, they had no more meaning to it than say a human might have for dead grass, leaves and shrubs that could surround such a human.

Absolutely of no consequence.

It had no more regard for the pathologist presently in charge of the morgue, as except for his human shape there was nothing to connect him to previous experience, or previous humans Creature encountered.

Incidentally, humans were almost as strange to Creature as *it* was to them, and except for Judy, Colleen and Frank, it had no specific feeling for any of them.

So, it pondered on the future for itself, and, indeed, the next step it should take in this *new* world.

It knew that it was extremely vulnerable to all of the world around it. And yet, it felt an urge to progress in life along any links it may possess, including the taking of risks. Just guessing, one might expect this trend due to the many situations it has survived by reason of its curiosity and innate sense of adventure........all along its life.

So, what now?

Creature, as an octopus might, crept over the edge of the drawer, then down to the floor. In doing this, it also discovered abilities it, itself, did not previously recognise it had.

It then propelled itself along the floor, to the exit to the morgue. For what reason, it did not yet know. Something in itself drove it to all these ventures. In the past, it always had humans to prompt it. And to look after it. But now, it realised it was on its own.

It crept out through the front door, awaiting the opportunity to move out past the revolving doors and when judging it safe.

Outside, there was traffic reminiscent of its escape with Colleen and Frank from the car-park in Darwin, and then the streets of Brisbane.

It then plastered itself onto the sidelight bordering the revolving glass door, and stayed there, considering its options.

It felt hungry. In the past, it could emanate this feeling to Colleen, and be rewarded with a feed of sorts, but no longer.

It, truly, was on its own.

So whereas before it could rely on Colleen feeding it through the special ports in its sphere, Colleen was no longer on the scene.

But it needed food.

It needed sustenance. Like we all do.

What to do?

As it stayed plastered on the glass sidelight, feelings totally alien to it arose in its consciousness. Sensing the presence of passers-by outside the morgue, strange emotions arose in Creature. Never before had it looked upon humans as a source of food, yet it now realised that humans were possessors of protein, carbs and other food-value things.

But apart from all that, now, noting the multitude of humans around it, milling around on the street outside the morgue, new feelings arose in Creature. The feelings were of *extreme hunger.*

And of course 'hunger' meant the need of sustenance from humans, and all other entities requiring the conversion of substances into living matter.

And so, our Creature started the feeling of the need of sources of protein and other matters we all take for granted. Before, all things were available to it; it was now open to all matters of existence. Now, it experienced actual *hunger,* as it really felt.

And that feeling resulted in not just hunger for any living thing. No longer hidden behind a veil of other things, it now felt it needed to *predate.*

It had no idea as to why this feeling arose in it for the first time after all the period of being without it.

But, there it was. No way could Creature define that it has perhaps *evolved* from a being classed by Jim Mullens as a mongrel dog.

But there was no question. *It has in fact evolved.*

And now, it saw, for the first time, all the people milling about it as *food.*

When the first wave of the new emotion hit it, Creature was alarmed, even horrified, experiencing self-reproach to allow such a feeling to permeate its usually placid *self.*

How can it experience such feelings, even desires, involving people? It could not comprehend the new view.

Then, as a little time passed, its hunger grew. And, again as time passed, its perspective subtly changed.

The people milling around on the street took on a new role. As a farmer may view his sheep, fond as he may have been of them, as food for the Sunday dinner, Creature began to view the humans within its vision the same.

An impersonal view, again strange to it, gradually fading into an even stronger feeling of extreme gripping hunger, such as a predator may experience.

All of a sudden, it could relate to the feelings of the entity that selected *Hans* as a prey (see volume II of this trilogy, or rather *by now* maybe 'tetralogy.').

It could presently sense humanity as prey.

The Entity has right now turned into a true monster.

As it crept around the building façade, it gradually fully changed into a *predator*.

And a predator needs food. Living food. Living protein.

And a predator nearly always selects its prey from the *weakest* members of its prey-herd. That is in-built into the DNA of the predator. Select the weakest and the youngest.

Creature crept around the corner near the morgue. And here, it spotted a smallish shape, a young girl, and its instincts told it that this was a safe prey.

And so it pounced.

The girl noticed the strange shape hurtling towards her. In sudden fear and disbelief, she momentarily froze in her tracks.

A bad mistake, but she was only a child. And Creature found its mark.

THE LOCAL POLICE WERE informed of the body found at the entrance of the lane by local residents.

By this time, Commissioner of the Australian Federal Police, Bill Bradbury, has also been informed of the breach in security of the ASIS-ASIO morgue.

The Federal Agents and the local police soon joined forces to disentangle the horrible chain of events that was thrust upon them.

The body found at the junction of the main road and the side-lane had been taken to the City Morgue, distinct from the ASIS-ASIO Morgue that originally housed Creature.

Here, the Government Pathologist was daunted by the condition of the corpse, and the probable crime that had been discovered.

The body did not give up any real clues as to the lead-up to its death. The cause of death itself was a mystery, along with the matter of '*how*'. '

The corpse seemed to have been sucked clear of of vitality, but only partially, above the shoulders.

The rest of the child was as perfect as it was only hours ago.

But above the shoulders, it was like the shrivelled and unwrapped remains of a mummy.

Or the whole presentation like an image of ancient Egyptian funerary gods; human bodies but a different, although in this case not an animal, head.

CREATURE FELT A MIXTURE of many emotions, a feeling of having done wrong, mixed with one of regret, then with another feeling, one of contentment at the release of hunger.

Through its erstwhile contacts with humans, and having read many of Colleen's books, it acquired much knowledge of the emotional and intellectual mind-processes of humans. It now faced conflict. And with conflict, came a flood of self-awareness. Was what it had done a criminal, even horrific, deed?

It could appreciate the evil overtones of its action. But what could it do, it asked itself, it had to survive. Which it could not do without food.

So, without actually understanding the process, it rationalised its action.

Yes, dear Reader, like humans who have done wrong, it justified what it did with a perfectly plausible explanation.

It had to do all that preceded, in order to stay *alive*. The prime incentive in all living things.

Survival of the fittest, if one could refer to the logic of Charles Darwin. And as much as some of Darwin's work had by now been discredited, the principle of 'survival of the fittest' had not. It was as valid now as ever before.

The kid that provided food for Creature was just not the fittest. Sad for her. She just happened to be on the scene at the wrong time for her. The *right* time for Creature…

THE BODY TURNED OUT to be of the child of a ne'er-do-well family. This identification was the result of a local police-station report of a missing child.

The mother, although poor, was caring. She reported the event of the missing child, the night before. The girl was a part-time employee of a low-level food chain, and on this night, she was rostered to fill in for the absence of a permanent employee, who happened to report ill.

The sick employee may have considered herself fortunate, as events turned out.

Certainly, she may have been the victim of this unparalleled attack, otherwise.

THE CITY POLICE HAD an unenviable task. No precedents (as was the usual case in criminal matters), no obvious motives, the child did not even have a boy-friend.

The few girls who were friendly to her, could offer no clues. Chloe, the child, left no evidence of any substance. She was simply walking home, and maybe 8.00 in the evening, not more than three blocks from her work-place, when she fell prey to an obviously evil predator. The identity of whom could not be imagined by the local police.

When Bill Bradbury arrived at the Police Station the next morning, he met a scene of total confusion. The horrific event could not be attributed to anyone from the local community. No such occasion could be found recorded in local records, nor in the records of adjoining precincts.

But of course, Bill had a clue. His long-standing adversary, Creature, fitted the role, although much remained to be explained.

Bill ordered a full autopsy, in bio-hazard conditions. But this gave no more clues to the event; the child was attacked by an unknown and indescribable entity, the attack was not observed, and the result was fast and total desiccation of the upper regions of her anatomy.

Bradbury called a meeting of the law enforcement management of all precincts in the general area. Added to this group were officers of the SAS, including all that took part in the capture of Creature. Also, he included the ASIS-ASIO Morgue Examiner, who had in the meantime suffered a goodly caning from his superiors for having allowed Creature to escape from the Morgue. And who died since. We won't forget Joe

Kadas, whose experiences at the Signals Directorate at Marainga and Pine Gap, were very relevant to Creature's career

Not that the Pathologist above had any choice in the matter; Creature's powers had not been published in the relevant Government Gazette as yet. But even if he had been warned, it was doubtful that he would have been able to resist the mental manipulation of Creature.

Bill opened the meeting by introducing extracts from previous events involving Creature, and also the episode of Hans (Onco II). These events were depicted on video image, as were some images of the 'kuru' incident. These latter were quite confronting, as for example the ritual eating by natives of the brains of a dead relative.

Let it be said that all these events, except for the 'kuru' one, gave a sufficient background of the power of Creature and associated matters. And even the 'kuru' case was a result of the Onco process, some saying that 'Onco the food' was a cousin of Creature.

Bill then tabled many of the events surrounding Colleen and Frank's escapades in recent times, whilst evading capture with Creature.

The closing part of the presentation was the rather gruesome shots of the victim of the recent attack.

Bill's closing words were; 'we have here a monstrosity beyond anything before encountered. We must all make an effort above anything else to capture or eliminate this being.'

'This includes law enforcement measures involving protection of the public, and in this respect some form of public announcement via the press and television may be appropriate, so long as it does not arouse panic.' He undertook to draft such an announcement.

With that, the meeting was closed, with Bill ensuring that all had his 24/7 phone link for emergencies.

CREATURE FELT THAT ITS new-found freedom was exhilarating. The traces of guilt for its gruesome deed slowly abated, as it further rationalised the event by cloaking it with the attitude of; 'the same as any other living being, I have the right to survive.'

And with that reasoning, Creature, without realising this in rational thinking, reached the threshold which tipped it into the realm of *total* monstrosity.

All the moral training by Colleen and Frank went up in smoke. All the events of cordial contact with humans went with it. As did all the self-education it managed to absorb whilst in the Weapons Development Dungeon.

Creature evolved into the unimaginable, and it was no longer a rational being in human terms.

Perhaps it did not realise, but all of this removed it from the safe envelope provided by Colleen and Frank. It was on its own, and could expect no help nor protection as of the time it left the ASIS-ASIO Morgue.

For three days it eluded all attempts to track it down. Hiding in rooftop down-pipes, else plastering itself up on the ceiling of underpasses, and other places its instincts urged to target, it once again felt the pain of hunger.

Acting on its previous experience, it again sought places where humans aggregated, being mindful of its natural caution.

IT LOCATED ITSELF IN a lane not far from its previous attack, high above the street, this time adhering to the underside of a pole-mounted transformer box.

There it remained, waiting for a prospective victim.

Until a stray dog happened to canter under the pole.

Creature has never seen a live dog before, but it came across references in the internet pages Colleen had allowed it to access.

It's instincts aroused, Creature contemplated whether to attack, or wait for a more suitable prey, such as a human, to come along.

It found that it's feeling of hunger, when aroused, was almost impossible to curtail.

So, without further consideration, Creature pounced on the hapless canine, again targeting the organ responsible for thought or feelings, or rather the casing of that organ, the skull.

The unfortunate animal was completely surprised by the attack, and it whimpered just a little, the whimper being completely ignored by the predator.

Creature had no compassion for the dog; it was just food, a source of protein.

The event was over in 3-4 minutes, and Creature, temporarily satisfied, clambered back up the pole, once again adapting the camouflage provided by blending into the colour of the transformer.

Creature was not truly assuaged by the meagre food value it gained in the attack, but it figured a little is better than nothing.

Two days later, it struck again, this time a young boy, who was despatched with the same cruelty at was the young girl earlier. The same modus operandi, it seemed that his face, together with the rest of his head, was sucked dry of all life, and the remains contained only a desiccated parody of the previous features and organs. Like a mummy.

AFTER THE MEETING WITH the relevant players at Canberra, Bill Bradbury returned to his abode in Adelaide, and after a hefty scotch (which was a rare event as Bill was not actually a drinker), he spent a little time with his family before retiring.

He had a really restless night, including some nightmares relating to Creature which caused him to wake in a cold sweat. His wife also was not immune, she also had some nightmares.

And at one point, Bill, upon waking, realised that he missed perhaps the most important item whilst in the meeting at Canberra.

Creature's ability to shed infectious cancer cells randomly releasing these into the world around it!

My God! He was all of a sudden in a panic, which again was unusual to Bill. He was normally calm and collected, even when facing extreme danger. And then he realised that it was not for himself that the panic arose. No, it was for the population of innocent souls......and he felt he had let them down, by overlooking a most important item.

The realisation came around 4.00 am, ACDT (Australian Central Daylight Time).

Bill knew there was not a minute to spare. He immediately placed a series of calls to all the attendees of the Canberra meeting, and was rewarded by shocked response from all.

Bill also alerted the Minister for Health at his home number, and spent a while explaining to him the panic he felt. The Minister was not ignorant of the health issues, he was well aware of the saga of Creature, as were by now all Cabinet Ministers.

Bill also immediately contacted ASIS and the local law-enforcement authorities, and requested that they quarantine the ASIS morgue, which housed the fugitive before it made good its escape.

The spectre of a national pandemic was something that could not be ignored, and the Minister, without concerning himself with the time of day, immediately called the Prime Minister.

The latter, also with no regard for niceties, aroused his secretary from sleep, and ordered her to immediately contact all members of the cabinet, and also the Leader of the Opposition (being the Alternative Prime Minister), and convene a bi-partisan meeting on a 'National emergency' basis, for the next day, at Canberra.

And so the insignificant cancerous growth managed to throw the nation into a state of terror.

BRADBURY REALISED THAT HE was outgunned in the matter. He soon held another meeting with the Minister for Health, and strongly advised him that help was needed if a cataclysm was to be averted.

The Minister said; 'what do you suggest, Bill?' The latter responded by putting the Minister in the picture concerning the roles played by Colleen Sans, Judy Hewitt, and Frank Vagyoczki.

He said he judged the matter to be serious enough to suggest to the Government that these persons be brought together and a task force be forged. He thought the task force should include the Minister for Health, to keep the focus on the health aspect.

He said; 'we don't need a highly virulent strain of cancer to rampage through the population. The thought of the carnage that could decimate the people out there was too horrible to contemplate. I am approaching you, Minister, on the basis of health. Other matters here are political and military, but in my opinion, the 'health' aspect is the most worrying and the most urgent.'

'I would ask that you approach the Prime Minister in order to get the authority for convening the main players, and since these people are in various Government departments, the Prime Minister is the only single authority that could bring them all together.'

Bill went on to say; 'Creature is able to shed highly virulent cancer cells without effort or will, it's just a natural state of its existence. All living beings shed some of their skin, the epidermis, and their hair constantly, and I don't wish to offend you with matters of which you are far more cognisant than I.' (The Minister was a fully qualified Medial Practitioner before entering Parliament, although due to his extreme age it might be doubtful if he would still remember his Hippocratic Oath).

'I will just add that whilst of course the shedding of epidermis in normal populations does not pose a threat to the average person, the same originating from *our* adversary is most dangerous.'

The Minister, Con Pappas, although ignorant of the particulars surrounding Creature's development, was well aware of the ramifications of the picture Bill was painting. He had no argument at all, and undertook to put the matter to Cabinet and so the Prime Minister at the next party meeting, which, as it happens, was only two days away.

JUDY HEWITT, COLLEEN SANS, and Frank Vagyoczki sat across each other at the Prime Minister's conference room in Canberra. Each has been personally requested by their respective superiors to attend, and all matters such as flights, accommodation, transport and meals were sorted out by the Prime Minister's Secretary.

All were provided with air tickets, hotel vouchers, specific Credit Cards, and all relevant items and each was given a special account on which to draw for whatever else they required during their stay in the Nation's Capital.

The night before, Colleen had a dream which was almost like a premonition; she dreamed she was again in a chopper approaching the geodesic polyhedron structures at the Maralinga Signals Directorate, when one of the radomes split open and Creature emerged, then clamped a tentacle around the helicopter, with the other appendages anchoring it to the dome. It then tried to pull the chopper down to the ground. She woke in a sweat, and then heard the phone ring. Amazing co-incidence, (or was it fate?); it was Bill Bradbury giving her advance notice of the requirement that she attend at Canberra.

Colleen said; 'Well, Judy and Frank, who could have seen this scene a year ago?'

Judy responded; 'No-one with any sanity could have forecast this a year or any number of years ago.'

Frank adjoined; 'I think a year ago I was patrolling the desert, and sleeping under canvas. You should see the apartment I have now.'

Just to fill the reader in on the events since Colleen and Frank's capture; most unusual, but they were allowed to lead their usual life in their old postings. Colleen and Frank kept up the relationship they enjoyed during the hectic chase from Maralinga to Darwin to Brisbane. As we will recall, they have become lovers, and remained so in spite of all the difficulties.

Judy was the same as before, although naturally a little older. John Boros had retired, and Judy was then elevated to Deputy Director, assisting Brian.

And so *here* they were again.

The three were chatting, waiting for Bill Bradbury, the Prime Minister, the Health Minister and the Leader of the Opposition. And whoever else may have been recruited by Bill.

CREATURE WAS, ONCE AGAIN, on the prowl. Emboldened by its previous success in hunting down three living beings, the little girl, the boy and the dog, it was now again hunting.

Colleen would have been shocked to see it now; when she last saw it, it was a kind of lovable being. As she then said; 'like a teacup poodle.' Now, it started to look evil. There was a kind of savagery emanating from it, and it was getting worse daily.

It maintained its preying position up the light pole, and under the pole-mounted transformer, and was scanning the street below for a likely victim.

It had by now grown quite a bit, probably weighing three kilos or so.

There was a derelict building across the street. It was the haunt of vagabonds, mostly homeless men, who used it as a place to crash after an alcohol or drug-filled night, or else a place to shelter in the rain. The local kids called it 'the Vampire house', and considering the activities that were soon to happen, it was not really a misnomer.

Creature wondered why it hadn't thought of it as an item of interest earlier; it sure would have been more comfortable than the transformer pole, and it could keep Creature out of sight easier. Plus, with the derelicts crashing there, there was a tempting source of food. Now, its interest kindled, it waited for the evening, when it could scuttle across the road unobserved.

Apart from having grown considerably, Creature also changed in appearance. Its vertices elongated, and it was growing three more from the soft areas on the sides of its body.

It was actually beginning to look more like an octopus than anything else, having by now eight appendages of one sort or another instead of the former five. This made the scuttling mode of its movement much more efficient. The major difference in appearance as an octopus was the absence of eyes or other interruptions in the smooth body of the monstrosity.

In any case, when night fell, it noted the reduction in the traffic volume, and in pedestrian density. It judged it was time to move.

It scuttled down the pole, and across the lane, and had no trouble in entering the old, rambling cottage. Unoccupied at the time as hoboes usually turned up later, Creature soon found a likely site of accommodation, in one of the few remaining cupboards in the erstwhile kitchen.

It then made itself comfortable, after devouring a stray rat, and waited for whatever was to happen.

The reader may wonder how it, being featureless, no mouth, could *actually* devour anything. This happened to be later the subject of discussion of the group in the Prime Minister's suite.

THE MINISTER FOR HEALTH and the Prime Minister arrived simultaneously, followed seconds later by Bill Bradbury and the

Opposition Leader, the latter having been briefed by Bill on the current situation.

It should be noted that the reason the Opposition Leader was included was that in such dire situations, if the Prime Minister became disabled for whatever possible reason, the Governor would appoint the Opposition Leader as caretaker Head of Government. Keeping in mind also that usually the Deputy P.M. would step into the role, but she was in hospital seriously ill with carcinoma of the lung.

After introductions, the Prime Minister opened with the statement; 'Friends, we are here for one very special reason (friends? Judy almost could not believe her ears. *This* from the Prime Minister of the Nation? To *her*, amongst the others?).

'That reason, continued the P.M., is that monstrous creature which is eluding interception, or capture, and which has unleashed fear, even terror, among the citizens of this State.

As you know, this entity has been laboratory-grown from a bunch of stem and specialised cancer cells, and in eluding capture, has sown the seeds, so to speak, of cancer which have already claimed a number of victims. Some of these are already dead, and others are isolated in the contagious diseases unit of Canberra Hospital.'

'The last person alive who actually *saw* this monster was the Pathologist at the morgue, and he died just days after Creature was released by him. His remains have been cremated', the same as the girl and boy that were found on the street after attacks by Creature. The dog that was also attacked was thrown into a wheelie-bin by a passer-by, and the latter also since turned up at the hospital.

There are presently four people in the segregation ward.

No trace of Creature. The area around the attacks was scoured and searched, including the derelict house, with no success.'

(Who would have thought of searching the little overhead *kitchen cabinet* for a fugitive murderer? Hmm?)

The six participants of the meeting spent the day and half the evening in discussing and planning the next move. Many initiatives were put forth, discussed, and discarded.

The P.M. questioned the ability of Creature to suck the heads and upper bodies of the victims virtually dry, when no one had ever seen any aperture such as a mouth on it?

Colleen responded; 'it absorbs things via a kind of osmosis, or else reverse osmosis. I have not yet figured out the precise method. Its surface is a porous, semi-permeable membrane, and it is extremely adept at absorbing through it. When I used to feed it, I would just squirt nutrient into its container, and you could almost see the nutrient mist get sucked into its surface.'

Perhaps about 7.00 pm the group broke up without reaching any particular resolution, and agreed to reconvene the next morning.

It may have been conventional that after such an arduous day, the participants may have a dinner or such like together.

However Colleen, with the others, decided to forgo this and get some sleep instead.

Soon, on a whim, Colleen herself decided to go for a little stroll before wrapping the night up, and she wandered about, deeply in thought, until all of a sudden….

She heard her name called;

"Colleen"

She looked about, but the streets were deserted, and she thought she was imagining things.

"Colleen"

Then she saw it. Like a shadow, amorphous against the trunk of a street tree.

'CREATURE!'

Colleen impulsively reached out towards the monstrosity. Then Creature emitted; 'No, no, Colleen, don't come near me. I don't want you to be harmed. I am dangerous.'

Colleen recoiled. For a moment, she was trapped in the past, where Creature was a lovable if unpredictable entity. Now? She realised she was in danger. But it was a tug-of-war. She still somehow cared for Creature, much like another innocent person often inexplicably cares for a violent criminal. Human nature?

'Creature, I know you would not hurt me. Please don't withdraw. Maybe we could find a place for you, where you would not do the abominable things they are accusing you of, right now.'

Creature responded; 'it's no good, Colleen. Perhaps before all this happened? But not any longer. There is no redemption for me anymore. I know they are hunting me, and one day they will corner me. And I can no longer rationalise any of this. I am what they say. In human terms, I am a *monster now unmasked.*

And the quicker all of this comes to an end, the better. I have no respect for myself, and no one else can ever replace the good feelings I once had. Even looking at you, now, along with the very caring emotions, I feel an urge in me to attack, to feed."

Goodbye, Colleen.'

And with a rustle of tree leaves, it was gone.

Colleen broke down. Sitting on a nearby bench, she sobbed her heart out. 'How can anyone have feelings for such an abomination?' She wept uncontrollably.

Then she got hold of herself. She directed a glance at the nearby trees, but there was no more movement nor shadows other than the bushy branches themselves, stirred only by the mild breeze.

She, without further ado, struck out for her hotel. Saddened, but realising that nothing could be done for Creature. Life had to take its course.

COLLEEN'S ROOM WAS ADJOINING Frank's. When she arrived back from her walk, she knocked on the adjoining door.

Frank responded with a worried look on his face. Hugging her close to him, he asked;

'Where have you been, honey? I've been worried about you! You're not familiar with Canberra.'

Colleen then told him of her unexpected encounter with Creature. 'Who would have thought that in a city with a million inhabitants, I would come across Creature. But Frank, it was very careful to avoid getting too close to me. And when I made an unexpected move towards it, I was met with genuine concern. It emitted, words to the effect; 'don't get close to me. You may be harmed. I am dangerous.'

Frank said; 'do you think that it was careful not to infect you? Or do you think it was to protect you from its predatory urges?

Colleen; 'I think a bit of both. It obviously regards itself as dangerous. More, it is clearly feeling guilty, ashamed, I would say.

Frank responded 'I hear you, but I don't think we can take any chances. At least it will be something to talk about, at the next meeting. Well, I am going to have a shower. Want to join me?

Colleen said; 'Not in the mood.' Then; 'Okay, but give me a minute to get myself together. I am a bit shaken by the encounter. Better yet, I will have a small scotch and then I will join you. Do you want a drink?'

Frank promptly agreed, and they sat around for a few minutes talking more around the episode Colleen had.

Colleen was the first to finish her drink, and she stood up and started undressing. Frank did not miss the opportunity to admire her, especially when she finished and stood stark naked before modestly throwing a towel about herself.

She threw that off before getting under the water, and invited Frank who did not really need an invitation. The shower was a twin design, ample room for them both. Frank got in, and asked Colleen if she wanted he back washed, and she readily agreed.

They washed each other, and Frank's reaction to all this was amply demonstrated by his bold erection. And Colleen was not backward, she dropped to her knees and started sucking Frank's penis.

It may seem incongruous that at times like the present, human beings could engage in sex-play. But the release from nervous tension is instant.

And one must remember the terrible things, wars and plagues like for example the Black Death between 1347 and 1351 with up to 200,000 deaths. Humanity still managed to keep copulating and procreating amongst all the horror and suffering.

So our couple were soon entwined on Frank's king-sized bed, and then, right when Colleen was reaching climax, Frank suddenly exclaimed; 'This is definitely the wrong moment, but the thought just came to me, out of nowhere: We must tell Bill Bradbury about your encounter. And you need to explain to him the area where Creature approached you. They are still fervently trying to find it, so it's urgent.'

Sorry, Colleen, but this must come before pleasure.'

Colleen was already on her feet, and in spite of the state of her emotions, she immediately agreed.

They rang Bill on his confidential mobile, and he answered after only a couple of rings. Colleen explained to Bill all that happened (*of course*, she did not include the shower episode), and she described to him the general area of the encounter. She did not know Canberra well enough to be more precise, but Bill soon got enough information out of her based on her responses to his specific questions. He located her on the edge of the Mt. Ainslie reserve, close to the National War Memorial.

That was enough for Bill. The scrub Colleen described was the reserve, and it meant that Creature had abandoned the area around the ASIS-ASIO Morgue, and struck out for better hunting grounds. Bill soon had a contingent of the AFP Special Response Group encircling the reserve, and he organised the ADF (Australian Defence Forces) to supplement Bill's troops.

The Army supplement brought with them mobile searchlights, and these were soon established all around the reserve, pointing their beams towards the centre of this.

Bill also mobilised an AFP helicopter, equipped for night work, that could hover over the woods with its laser guided search-light as well as its infra-red body-heat detecting sensors, aimed on the bush.

During the conversation with Bill, Frank naturally enough wilted, but when Bill left the phone, Colleen soon made sure that Frank was ready for some more play.

So the earlier climax was soon resumed, and our couple had a good time which they appreciated. And, they had been so tense lately, any relief from stress was more than welcome.

Colleen chose that she would spend he rest of the night with Frank, and instructed the Night Clerk to redirect any calls that may come in for her to Frank's room.

Her and Frank decided to watch TV for just a little while, ad when they switched on the set, there were news bulletins in progress. News reporters were already covering the events at the Reserve, and TV coverage was of course inevitable.

The multitude of police and armed services personnel were clearly shown in the newscasts. These personnel all wore white bio-suits, fully covering them from head to toe. In the beams of the search lights they could be seen moving around the shrub, like wandering ghosts.

Meanwhile, like a pack of wolves, the reporters on site were crowding the police seeking information on *just what was happening.*

But the police were tight-lipped. They had strict orders as to confidentiality

But no one as yet knew the reason for the commotion, nor whom it was that the Authorities were chasing. Creature was still a secret, but as Bill was well aware, the cat was busy working its way out of the bag. It was only a matter of time.

When the newscast went off-air, Colleen and Frank shared a well-earned if short rest. Till the clock-alarm went off at 7.00 a.m.

Then, they got up and showered again -no game playing like last night,- went down for breakfast, and by the time all this was over, it was time to again meet the Prime Minister.

The meeting chaired by the Prime Minister resumed that day. It was getting to be a largish group, more than was originally envisaged.

The importance and the urgency of the proceedings were well demonstrated.

DURING THIS TIME, CREATURE kept ducking the Authorities. From tree to tree, from bush to bush, from dugout to dugout, it kept evading capture. It was also getting very hungry, which weakened its constitution.

It managed to corner a couple of rats, even a feral cat, but all this was not nearly enough. It was growing.

And it was hour by hour getting more distant from its previous human-like character, and slowly it was again becoming more like the being Jim Mullens dubbed a 'mongrel dog,' so long ago.

The Prime Minister's meeting got underway with the attendees now also aware of the incidents last night. Bill Bradbury was still the operational leader, whilst the P.M. held it all together, and imbued the political and public face into the congregation.

The P.M. opened the meeting declaring that he was contemplating initiatives for the establishment of a state of National Emergency. Bill Bradbury then ran a resume of the history of Creature. He informed the gathering of the imminent danger of Creature shedding free infectious cancer cells into the human population. The Minister for Health added his piece, fearing that a pandemic might be on the horizon.

The previous angle of Weapons Development was completely demolished, by decree of the P.M. He stated that the risk to humanity was far in excess of any benefit that Australian Weapons Development might gain by the use of Creature for such purposes. He also mentioned that the United Nations Convention on the ban on Biological Weapons (10 April 1972) was probably already breached by Australia in trying to develop Creature further for such purposes.

The P.M. then informed all that the current situation in Cabinet was that all members without exception voted for the 'death sentence' for Creature, effective immediately. And all relevant Government agencies were mobilised to carry out this sentence.

So, it was *'open season'* on Creature.

Bill himself recalled that he attended 'duck season' in the marshes around the city of Sale in Victoria, some time ago. The scenario here was reminiscent of that hunting adventure, though ducks were certainly not dangerous, but this organism *sure* was.

Colleen's heart sank on hearing all this. She was, for some unknown reason, still very fond of the entity. She cast her mind back to her original meeting with Creature. And all the events since. Even remembering her statement to it that if she could, she would hug it to her.

Oh, so much water passed under the bridge since those days.

The escape with Frank to Darwin, on the Ghan Railway, through Alice Springs with Creature dressed like a human baby in a basket, the clothes outside its acrylic globe.

The escapades with Gavin Hoffman and Brett Snellman, and the final capture of creature, apparently dead, then coming back to life in the ASIS-ASIO morgue.

Then the encounter at the edge of the bush the other night. All this almost too much for her to grasp, and she wondered how she got through all the exploits in one piece.

She was half listening to Bradbury and the P.M., with her mind still musing over the past.

CREATURE DETECTED THE BIO-HAZARD clad group of intruders into what it deemed as *its* bush. It was undecided as to what the best move was for it.

It was still hungry, and as far as it could, it supplemented its diet with small animals and insects, abundant in the bush. But, an insistent thought in its mind, human prey was what it craved.

And there it entered into conflict. Underneath it all, due to its exposure to and nursing by people, as such, particularly Colleen and Frank, it suddenly realised that it had developed a sense of affection for humans. *Certain* ones, to be sure.

And reciprocating they developed an affection for *it*. *What an enigma for Creature. You want to eat the people that nurtured you!*

Creature was in a complete dilemma. And then it thought, it may even be better to surrender itself and be free of all this conflict.

There was no way it could attack Colleen. But as for others, it had little compunction. And the only 'others' it could discern right now were the white-suited humans invading its current habitat. Protective suits and weapons. It had no feelings for them. They were hunting it, and when one was hunted, one could not feel affection.

In a couple of ways, it could no longer contain itself. So, it selected a human that unwisely strayed from the company of others, and waiting for a suitable moment, it pounced.

Due to the bio-suits, it could not penetrate to the body of its victim. But having had experience with acrylic barriers, it decided that the best approach was to attack the face-mask of the person, which was, of course, acrylic. But a hard form of this. Almost as glass.

So, Creature, on an impulse, launched at the person selected, and clamped its vertces onto his face mask. Then, it exerted as much pressure as it could, and finally the mask cracked. Immediately, it extended its vertices, or shall we by now call them tentacles, into the fractured plastic, and then embarked on its horrible endeavour to suck the life force out of its captive.

The man, in the interim, struggled and threshed around, trying to scream, but Creature, once it got hold of its victim, immediately began its feeding procedure. Continuing to drain its victim dry…

No-one in the past could figure out how a creature with no apertures in its presentation could emit what sounded like voices, receive what was sound, and feed on a live being.

No mouth.

No nose

No ears.

But it could still do all the things another being could do.

The feeding? As mentioned before, Creature <u>seemed</u> to use almost simple *osmosis* or *reverse osmosis, although these terms relate more to 'solute differential.'* It basically just sucked using the pressure diferential between its own substance and that of its victim, and so it obtained the nourishment it sought. So efficiently, that the victim became no more than a desiccated husk. In minutes.

So in our scenario at the present, it managed to do this in spite of the high-tech suit. And when the others of the search party found the victim, there was nothing that they could do for him. He was well and truly dead, like the others before.

The event was disclosed to the Government meeting in minutes, and the P.M., who has by now *finally* finished setting up a dedicated task-force, responded with alarm.

The task force presently met daily in order to keep abreast of the developments, and now had a very clear case of the unfortunate officer that was pounced upon.

This was the first time a law-enforcement person was attacked, and it did not go down well with Bill Bradbury, either.

Bill proposed an all-out blitz to capture or kill the entity. Now that it was well and truly located in the Ainsleigh Reserve bush area, Bill thought that it was time.

The P.M. could have no objection to this, as it was a logical conclusion, and in any case, cabinet had already decided upon this. The others in the Task Group also all agreed to this, even Colleen, who was at times hesitant to encourage moves to harm Creature.

It had gone too far

But Colleen asked to be excused of any direct action against the entity. She preferred to see herself in a more passive role instead.

The P.M. agreed, and it was the second time Colleen managed to be clear of Government intrusion. The first was still at the Weapons Development Dungeon, where she confronted, and successfully, the *then* Minister for Defence to avoid being body-searched.

Now how to terminate or capture Creature?

One suggestion was to cast a huge net over the bush. Another was to move ground-troops in a sweeping operation, combing through the bush at ground level, each bearing a pistol, and holding a cattle-prod, to poke into unreachable spots. Drones would scoop the tree-tops for any sign of the fugitive.

In the end, the latter option was approved by the P.M.

And so it happened.

CREATURE WAS MOVING THROUGH the bush, in an endeavour to capture any living thing. In its sweep through the scrub, it managed to catch a native bird, then a field mouse, then another feral cat. But, nothing of substance, except for the Officer. But that was already some little time ago.

It needed something bigger to appease its constant hunger.

And then, all of a sudden, it located some more of the white-clad humans, in protective clothing, approaching along a bush trail.

It immediately assumed its protective camouflage -as we know, like an octopus, it could change its appearance to blend in with the environment; in this case, the bush.

Then, it proceeded in selecting a suitable victim among the searchers. It was somewhat thwarted by the instructions of Bill Bradbury to his troops, that they should never separate and always stay together in this hunt.

However, it did select the most suitable among the group, and this was a female - not that Creature could tell - officer, smaller and slighter in stature than the others. Creature instantly located its attention to this person, and was carefully watching her to wait for some opportunity hoping she separated from the group.

As we said, Creature was well camouflaged this time in mottled green, approximating the hues of the background scrub.

It slowly crept closer to its target, but was thwarted by the officer sticking close to the rest of his or her troop, as instructed. Creature then decided to present a ruse, by rustling in the undergrowth, not far from her feet. As it hoped, the officer turned towards the disturbance, and was actually approaching Creature. What could be better, it thought.

As it coiled its tentacles for the attack, the officer turned fully front-on. And, with a shock, Creature realised it was Colleen. Creature also noticed that unlike the others, she did not have a gun, nor a cattle prod.

She was only there as an observer, not a hunter.

Creature was shocked. Its instinct was to strike, but something inside it made it pause.

Confusion!

At the same time, Colleen spotted Creature. How? It was so that in its confusion, Creature dropped the camouflage. It immediately and automatically reverted to its natural shade of pink. And as it was right in front of Colleen, the latter was in shock due to the sudden appearance of Creature, apparently out of nowhere.

'Creature!' she exclaimed. 'Colleen' it emitted.

The officers close to Colleen could not help but hear her speak. And the responding 'Colleen' would have been also clear enough for them to detect, but they didn't sense this, due to the electronic shielding each now wore.

A group of officers immediately surrounded Colleen and Creature, and although Creature immediately emitted a mental attack ordering the troops to drop their weapons, they did not.

As this manoeuvre always worked before, Creature became even more confused, and also afraid.

Then, at this moment, a drone appeared overhead, swooping fairly close above the group. Back at the temporary Control Room, Bill Bradbury happened to be sitting in the Controller's chair, in front of the monitors.

The drone was equipped with a single rocket propelled grenade, and viewing and targeting apparatus to match.

Bill said, through gritted teeth, 'got you, you bastard!' And as the fugitive appeared on target and in range, Bill flicked the switch safety hood off, and hit the firing button.

From a distance of perhaps 12 metres, the rocket left the drone and in a split second, found its target. Or near enough.

At the same time the drone sounded a 'whoop-whoop' siren, triggered by the dropping grenade, and having been trained in the procedures, all the officers scattered in all directions. In this case to escape he effects of an explosion.

With all its formidable defences, Creature had no protection. The rocket hit the ground centimetres from its body, and blew a ragged hole in the soil. The sudden explosion blasted Creature a couple of metres above the terrain. The shock wave was almost enough to kill a human at that distance, and Creature, either killed or stunned, fell and lay like a limp rag on the surface.

Then, Bill from the loudspeaker in the drone; 'keep clear, people. The beast is still dangerous.'

And his Operations Manager at the Control Room immediately set the pre-planned action into motion.

The Attack Team was scrambled, and boarded a low-downdraft Apache AH-64S combat helicopter. All the officers on the ground had PLB's (Personal Locator Beacons) which are really position report emitters transmitting at 406 MHZ on their person, and the chopper made a bee-line to the site.

Within a very short time, it was hovering over the blast area, and armed personnel were lowered via aerial lines.

Equipped with full bio-suits, and all weaponry necessary, the troops gathered the remains of Creature into a bio-container, using a remotely operated mechanical clasp. The question of whether the remains contained any signs of life, or not, was left to the forensic scientists at ASIO.

The whole complete item was speedily flown to ASIO headquarters. Specifically, the Intelligent Life division. This division also handled information relating to the international programme for SETI, or *'Search for Extra-Terrestrial Life'*.

Not that anything like that has ever been encountered….to the present. But it seemed to be the most appropriate Department.

And all this as per the protocol for handling threatening life forms. Creature in its container was deposited at the ASIO-ASIS Establishment in Canberra, awaiting analysis.

All under the highest security standard in the land.

Bill Bradbury could not contain his curiosity. After all the time hunting it, it had finally come within his grasp. So, taking advantage of his high level security clearance, he visited the lab.

The container, which was refrigerated, had been depressurised to negative atmospheric value, a mild vacuum, and had a transparent panel. It was easy to view the prisoner without direct contact, and Bill made sure that all was according to rules and regulations.

And as he surveyed the captive, dead or alive, he could experience a feeling of unease. No reason that he could detect. Just a feeling. Maybe all the terrible things that have happened? Or was it that in the past, all things about Creature were a shock. Or at least a surprise.

In the laboratory itself, the scientific staff shared these feelings. For some reason, anyone in the vicinity of the container could feel the same unease that Bill felt.

The Prime Minister's meeting was reconvened, and all were briefed concerning the current situation.

There were still some questions.

How was it possible that Creature had previously demonstrated its ability for telekinesis, and for psychic communication, and yet it did not appear to use such powers when its life was at risk, during its capture in Canberra?

The Minister for Health (whose portfolio included other scientific matters) reported that the CSIRO, the Commonwealth Science and Industrial Research Organisation, was recently successful in producing an electromagnetic radiation emitter which scrambled rays like X-rays and radar and radio transmission and similar and rendered them ineffective. Hopefully this applied also to mental emissions.

Bill Bradbury then reported that scrambling emitters had been obtained from CSIRO and were issued to the ground troops searching for Creature. It was obvious to Bill that the emitters did the job they were supposed to do.

'Proof of the pudding', he said enigmatically, 'was eating it.' So whatever Creature might have tried during its capture had no further effect on people around it.

The conference was then disbanded by the P.M., except he asked Bradbury to keep Colleen and Frank at Canberra for a few days. Just in case.

THE QUESTION AROSE ON the subject of just what to do with Creature. It appeared dead, and the Director in charge of the ASIS lab recommended destruction.

Nobody argued about this, but the matter needed resolution as to the method of disposal. Dead or alive, Creature proved to be a continuing problem.

Technical Advisors suggested that the entire container including the terror should be placed into the High Temperature Incinerator at St. Peters, a Sydney suburb. This incinerator was used routinely to dispose of dangerous materials by Government Departments, and was used also by large hospitals handling infectious disease waste.

(This Incinerator was built to a quality exceeding that of the *European Waste Incineration Directive Standard* with many plants operating in Scandinavia and other places. The European Standard prescribes a minimum Flue Gas Temperature of 850 degrees Celsius or 1560 Fahrenheit for 2 seconds. The one at St. Peters was designed for 900 degrees Celsius for 2 seconds.).

The P.M. opted for this. He said; 'no heat is high enough for this horror. *Hell* would be the only other place, and we don't have access to that *as yet!*'

Of course, he was wrong in this as the core of the U.S. nuclear explosions at Hiroshima and Nagasaki in August 1945 might have been *600,000 degrees* Celsius.

At any rate, he gave direct instructions to Bill Bradbury. Bill had no problem complying.

BUT HOW TO? THE Strategic boffins in Defence drew up a plan of how to dispose of Creature. It, in its container, will be further packaged in a wooden crate, which would have attached to it an emission scrambling device the same as was used at Ainsleigh Reserve.

This was to ensure that Creature, had it in some way miraculously recovered, would have no power over any humans handling its cage.

The crate itself would be transported to St. Peters by armoured helicopter.

And so it happened. Upon arrival at the incinerator, the crate was placed on the feed-in to the moving grate.

There was no preliminary examination to ensure that Creature was dead. It would not have made any difference in either case.

The irony of the incineration process was not lost on Bill Bradbury, as a 'cousin' to Creature was similarly incinerated, although by flame-thrower, at Adelaide Hospital a long time ago (ONCO II).

The only possible loose end was that the buds that fell off Creature earlier were still in a refrigerated drawer at the morgue. The fact was that everyone forgot about them.

It would have ben better to incinerate them along with Creature.

At any rate, Creature lost its tenure on this planet, and Bill along with others breathed a sigh of relief when the call came from the Incinerator Control Room.

Just a brief message, which only stated to Bill; *'it is done.'* And that was the end of the most dangerous living being *ever* on Planet Earth.

OR WAS IT?

SOME WEEKS LATER, IT occurred to one of the Pathologists at ASIS-ASIO that the occupants of the refrigerated drawers of course rotated, a body being removed for post-mortem examinations, then that same drawer gaining a new occupant, in due course.

But as this Pathologist noticed, there was one drawer that was never opened. And the drawer was un-labelled.

So, on this day, he went and opened it.

Instead of a cadaver, as he expected, there was only a folded aluminium envelope, sealed with tape. Surprise would describe his feeling; 'something new every day,' he muttered to himself.

Not wishing to tread on someone's toes, he decided to leave the object in its place, till he could bounce it off his boss, the Senior Pathologist.

And so he did.

When the Senior Pathologist, Dr. Lao Wang, learned of the matter, he looked in the drawer for himself. He then decided to contact Bill Bradbury of the AFP whom he knew due to a former case where the corpse, of an AFP Officer, was being examined. As it sometimes happens in such matters, Bradbury and Wang struck up a cordial relationship.

Wang was an interesting person; born at Ürümqi, in the shade of the Tian Shan mountains (Mountains of Heaven), he was of Chinese parentage. Before completing his training, he travelled extensively in the surrounding countries, such as Kyrgyzstan, Tajikistan, Mongolia etc., and was well versed in the cultures of these and many other countries.

Bill Bradbury was a sort of kindred spirit, he also loved travelling in China and other Asian places.

So, Wang called Bradbury; 'Hi, Bill, this is Lao. We seem to have found some material which you may be aware of' (and he continued to relate the details as he knew them).

Bills response was; 'Bloody hell. I *know* what that package is. But me, along with everyone else, forgot about it being in the morgue. I could kick myself, and I won't be surprised if the Minister does just that when he finds out. Which he will, as I will have to inform him.'

'But more urgently, Lao, seeing that the item is located in your premises, I guess I have to ask you to proceed and examine the contents. Please treat this as a routine investigation, except that you must follow biological decontamination protocol. Isolate the area, until you can choose suitable personnel, and ensure any such persons wear full bio-suits.

'But wait, better than that, hold on for me. I will fly up from Adelaide, and join in the examination, not later than tomorrow. In the interim, ensure you label the drawer 'no access.' Make certain no-one interferes.'

And so it happened. Bill turned up the next day, after having had some strips ripped off him by the Minister for the ineptitude (the Minister's words) displayed. The Minister added; 'Will this Onco business *ever* come to end?

Lao Wang decided to continue handling the matter personally, after finding out about the Minister's involvement.

So, when Bill turned up the next day, they both donned bio-suits, and proceeded to remove the item from the drawer, then place it on a dissection table. Further using 'infectious diseases' protocol, they opened the aluminium envelope with a pair of sterile scissors. The contents were spilled into a sterile stainless steel kidney-dish, ready for examination.

They *still* looked like a pile of scorched dog-biscuits, and Bill was not sure if they had an element of life in them. *That* was the first priority to determine. But how? How would you determine if a mass of dog-biscuits has a spark of life? Lao went back to the elementary tenets of his B.Sc. Doctorate;

Requirements for signs of life;

- organization of cells.
- use energy.
- homeostasis.
- respond to their environment.
- growth and development.
- reproduction
- pass along hereditary traits.
- adapt to their environment.
- And a couple more provisions, not relevant here.

By using a true/false tick-sheet, there was found no sign of any factor signalling life.

However, Bill was not satisfied. He said to Lao; 'The originator of these objects led us up that many false trails and dead ends, that I really need something more positive.'

'Lao, take one of these and immerse in a sterile test-tube in warm sterile water, say 30 degrees Celsius. Allow 48 hours keeping constant temperature, and then review.

Especially note any change in density or shape.'

'Take another one, check for endothermic absorption

Is there any change upon being subjected to energy radiation?'

'Then, take another one again, place it on a nutrient slide, and record any change.

The rest, put back into refrigeration.'

For 48 hours, the ASIS Morgue remained closed. Any cadavers of ASIS-ASIO interest during this time were shunted to the City Morgue.

At the end of the period, an assessment of the situation was produced.

A review of all the procedures and results was made.

It was found that in spite of the relevant scientific procedures, no trace of life could be found.

Frank, at the earlier time, made a good job of attempting to terminate the prodigy, or whatever, of *Creature.*

Bill was finally free of the burden of worrying about any residue of Creature.

He then ordered all remnants of the procedures recently undertaken to be sent to St. Peters for incineration, after being encapsulated in a sterile container.

Next day, he got the customary curt return notice of the incineration having been performed.

This truly *must* have meant the end of ONCO!

And it did!

(Or did it? What about the ONCO food production line?)

Printed in the United States
By Bookmasters